Amish Sisters Marry

Dinah's Darling

Book 2

By Rose Doss

ISBN: 978-1-955945-52-3

Cover images courtesy of dreamstime
Interior image from Brandi Lea designs
Cover by Joleene Naylor.

Manufactured/Produced in the United States

CHAPTER ONE

"Is that your brother, Levi, I see over there?" Dinah tried not to look obvious, resisting the urge to point at the *Mann*. He looked like Levi, but she'd never seen Esther's brother look quite this serious. His expression was almost stern.

The Baumgartner living room had gotten warm with all the bodies there for the Sing and Dinah started fanning herself.

Of course, Levi Becker had moved away when he married, so she hadn't seen him in a number of years. She supposed a *Mann* whose wife had died would look serious, but hadn't Levi been widowed several years ago?

"*Yah*," Esther Becker said. "Remember that I've been working in Levi's shop with him?"

"Oh, yes," Dinah agreed. "You did say that. I've just not seen him at services."

The members of the congregation shifted as they moved out of the Becker *Haus*, most of the women heading to the kitchen to prepare lunch for the crowd.

Dinah went to make herself helpful and was assigned to pass out bread rolls to everyone seated at the tables. In moving through the group, she saw Levi Becker talking to a small bunch of *Menner*. Intent on her job, she didn't at first register that her sister, Abby, wasn't working with the kitchen crew or sitting a table.

Looking around eventually, she didn't see Abby anywhere.

Putting her empty breadbasket on the kitchen counter, Dinah passed through the room and went out the back door, looking for Abby.

Although her *Schweschder* wasn't a highly social girl, Abby knew all these folk and generally circulated freely among their friends.

Just as the thought surfaced in Dinah's head, she heard muffled sobs from around the kitchen corner. Her footsteps heading in that direction, it didn't even occur to her that whoever was crying in secret might not want to be discovered. She just wanted to help anyone in that distress.

Reaching the corner of the *Haus*, Dinah peeked around and saw in dismay that her sister stood behind a sheltering bush, weeping muffled sobs into her elbow.

"Abby!" She rushed to throw her arms around her sister. "Abby."

In all the time since Gabe's death, she'd only ever seen Abigail weep silent tears, tracking down her pale cheeks like bird prints in the snow. This was gulping, noisy sobs that her sister could only silence into her bent elbow.

"Whatever is the matter?" Dinah hurried to say against Abby's white *Kapp*.

"He said—he said—" Abby hiccupped, sniffing back tears.

"Who said?" Dinah demanded.

Abby shook her head, her tears having come to a stop. "Oh, nothing. It was nothing. I just overheard Levi Becker—you know, the *Mann* who was Gabe's friend—talking to some other *Menner*."

Her words subsided as she broke into a sob.

"What did Levi say? Did he say something to upset you?" Dinah spoke with indignation.

Abigail seemed to pull herself together, wiping her damp cheeks with the corner of her apron. "Nothing that's not true, but I don't see how any *Mann* would want to marry a woman who can't have babies."

"What did he say? Sister, what did Levi say? You're not this upset over nothing."

"It was nothing. Nothing." Abby's voice was stone cold as she scrubbed at her pale cheeks. "Certainly nothing to get into a tizzy over. What is true, is true."

"You don't cry over nothing," Dinah retorted.

Abby shook her head. "It was just…just that Levi talked of Gabe having died without having a child." A sob rose in her again and broke loose from her sister's throat.

Abby's face crumpled and she burst into tears as Dinah pulled her into a hug.

"I so wanted to have a child with Gabe! We had been married five years before he died in that accident!"

Dinah dragged in a breath. "Many women have children later. Don't cry, sister, and don't worry that no *Mann* will want to marry you."

The longer Abby grieved Gabe, though, Dinah had begun to wonder if her sister wanted a new husband.

Abigail drew a breath, clearly trying to calm herself. "I'm not crying now, Dinah. We can go in with the others."

"Are you sure," Dinah asked doubtfully.

"*Yah*." Her sister wiped her face again. "I was just surprised to hear it spoken. Levi Becker only said the truth. I've known for some time that I'm unlikely to marry again. What *Mann* wants a *Frau* who can't have *Bopplin*? Hearing it out loud…discussed openly by Levi. It surprised me. If any *Mann* had thought of marrying me, the truth is now clearly spoken. I can't have babies."

"That was a terrible thing to even mention! You're recently widowed," Dinah said hotly. "It's not been that long. I think even speaking of Gabe is wrong."

"I'm not that recently widowed and Gabe was Levi's friend when they were *Youngies*." Abigail's voice was cold again. "It's only natural that he should think of Gabe. I must face the truth. No *Mann* will want to marry a barren woman. I don't really want another husband anyway."

"I don't think he should have said such a thing," Dinah muttered, following Abby out of the shrubbery. "I can't forgive him so easily as you."

“I don’t care that Levi will be left tending his shop by himself when you marry and move away,” Dinah hissed to her best friend, Esther. “He may be your brother, but he’s a rude, cold *Mann* and he hurt my sister with his harsh words!”

The two girls sat on hard, ladder-backed chairs to the side of the Augsberger’s crowded living room. The community had come to worship there, two weeks after Dinah had found Abby weeping. The Augsberger place was crowded and buzzing with conversation as friends exchanged greetings. The service not having started, the hum of chatter filled the room.

Noise rose all around them.

“Please! Please! Please!” begged Esther quietly, her cherubic face pleading. “I know you’re looking for a job and Levi will need your help when I’m gone.”

Dinah stubbornly shook her head.

Esther shook her head despairingly. “Levi isn’t good at asking for help. I know a dozen of our neighbors would be glad to fill in, at least temporarily, but my *Bruder* willfully says he can manage alone and he needs someone to do the job for more than a day or two!”

“There!” Dinah declared with an edge of triumph, “he doesn’t even want to hire help.”

Esther grimaced in exasperation. “Oh, he knows he’ll have to have help eventually, but, like I said, he’s terrible at asking for it.”

Her friend’s jaw firmed and Dinah registered that Esther could be as stubborn as she’d been told she was. Their similarities had both drawn them together and caused their occasional tiffs.

“Look, Esther, I know you’re to marry Jakob Moser in a week and move away with him, but Levi is mean and unfriendly. He hurt Abby terribly. Do you think I’d have anything to do with the *Mann* who was the cause of grief for my beloved sister? Much less work with him.”

“I don’t know why he made that remark about Gabe. If ever a *Mann* was happy with his wife, it was Gabe Eichelberger. He had no complaints about not having had children yet.”

"Well, Levi shouldn't have embarrassed and hurt Abby by saying he did! And within her hearing when she was grieving Gabe."

"No, Levi shouldn't have said anything, but doesn't *Gott* recommend us to forgive?"

Dinah burned at the memory of holding a sobbing Abby in her arms. Competent, serene Abby didn't cry very often. As a matter of fact, Dinah thought she'd only seen this after Gabe's death and then again after Levi's horrible comment.

"I can't forgive Levi," she said in a hard voice. "I've even prayed about it. There's just no way I can work for him."

"Please, please, please?" Esther repeated. "He's my *Bruder*. I can't just get married to go off and leave him!"

"This is Levi's problem. Not yours."

"Would you say that if it was Adam?" Esther posed. "And think about Jakob. He so wants us to marry."

At the mention of her own brother, Dinah had to firm her facial expression. Esther knew how attached she was to her elder brother…and she had a point when she mentioned her soon-to-be husband. It wasn't really fair to Jakob that Esther wasn't able to commit to leaving Levi in the lurch.

"Did you ask Amity or Grace? Maybe one of them can do it." Her resolve weakening in face of her friend's desperate pleas, Dinah threw out the names of two other friends.

"*Yah*, of course, I did! Amity's taken Becca's job at the Sunflower Inn, now that Becca's married. Besides Levi won't work with Amity. He said she's dizzy. And Grace works making pies and canning jellies with her sister. They can neither take the job."

Esther reached out to take Dinah's hand. "Levi's not so bad, truly. He's perfectly nice. Remember that from before when we were growing up together? Once he gets to know you, he's lovely. He's gone through a rough patch since losing his wife several years ago, though, and that's made him seem more abrupt."

"Then, you'd think that his loss would have made him more sensitive to Abby!"

“Please, Dinah,” Esther said. “I’ve asked everyone and no one old enough for the job can take it.”

Dinah felt herself wavering even more at the sincere pleading note in her friend’s voice. “I can’t. He hurt Abby.”

“I’m not expecting you to have to work for him for a very long time,” Esther entreated. “I’m sure someone else, who Levi will work with, will become available to do it.”

“I’d have to talk to Abby.” Dinah swallowed, feeling backed into a corner. “I’m promising nothing. She’ll probably be very hurt at the suggestion.”

“Of course! Of course. She’s very reasonable, though,” Esther responded hopefully.

“Maybe.” Dinah just remembered her sister’s unusual bout of tearfulness.

She even hated to bring up the issue…but Esther was in a bad spot.

“Of course, you should take the job,” Abigail said calmly the next day, as she and Dinah unloaded bags from the Offenthaler grocery store.

Dinah stopped emptying the containers of flour and coffee, staring at her.

“What? But he hurt you! Levi said ugly things—right in your hearing—about Gabe having had to die childless.” She was astonished at her sister’s declaration.

“He did die childless,” her sister pointed out, still in that hard, level voice.

Dinah saw the flicker in Abigail’s gaze, though. She reached out to place her hand on Abby’s arm. *“Schweschder.* Sister. This is not your fault. It is *Gott* who opens or closes a woman’s womb.”

Abby said in a dry voice, “I don’t think we can blame *Gott* for this. He certainly can open a womb, but I think He only does good.

Maybe He knew that Gabe and I were better off not having children."

"No! Why you will make a wonderful mother! You were only married five years. If Gabe were still alive, you'd have many years of marriage for *Kinder*." Dinah said, then added in a venomous voice, "That cold snake, Levi Becker made out that it was your fault you and Gabe didn't have children! There's no way, I could work for him."

"Sister," Abigail said calmly, "you're looking for a job and Levi has need of a worker. Let his comment that day not deter you. Nor his demeanor. A boss doesn't have to be friendly. After all, he and Gabe were friends, both before he moved to marry and after he returned. Let us believe that Levi spoke out of grief that day, not true conviction."

Dinah considered her a moment. "You are too good. What Becca said about you is right."

Abby laughed. "Our younger sister is often right, but no one should think I'm perfect. All have sins."

"Name one of yours." Dinah went back to unloading the bags.

A wry smile quirked her lips. "I could give you lists, but these matters are between *Gott* and myself. He knows my struggles. I don't need to bare these to anyone!"

She disappeared into the pantry closet to stock shelves and Dinah watched her go.

Please, Lord, Dinah prayed. *Help me know what to do. I know Abby was more hurt by Levi's words than she lets on, but should I ignore this? Please help me. Should I work with this cold, unfriendly Mann?*

That evening after supper, Dinah and her younger sisters, Naomi and Faith, cleaned the kitchen as *Mamm* and *Grossmammi* sat nursing cups of coffee at the table. Abigail was out in the back garden with Ezra, their youngest brother.

"I think you should take the job with Levi Becker," announced *Grossmammie* in a contented voice. Dinah's dilemma had been a matter of talk within the family and all knew of Esther's plea since Dinah wasn't prone to keeping her troubles to herself.

"You have been looking for several weeks for a job," *Mamm* observed. "This might not be so bad."

"Not so bad," Dinah said hotly. "Maybe you've forgotten, *Mamm*, that Levi Becker is such an unpleasant *Mann.* He was the one who made that ugly remark about Gabe having died without any children. Made that comment where Abby could hear him! Besides, he's not at all approachable or warm."

"I haven't forgotten," her mother responded in a placid voice. "A boss doesn't need to be approachable or warm."

"Levi lost his wife and their child not that long ago," *Grossmammi* commented sadly. "It was only several years back."

"That's no excuse for his manner or his words!"

"*Neh*, my *Leibling*," her *Mamm* said. "It's not an excuse, but having lost his wife is a sadness."

"I still don't think I should work for him," Dinah said, stubbornness in her voice.

"Work is good for the soul and can make the *familye* stronger," Naomi spoke up to say.

"Of course, it's good," Dinah snapped. "That goes without saying, but working for this kind of *Mann?*"

Grossmammi took a drink before saying, "Abby told you she didn't care what he'd said."

"You actually asked her about this?" Faith inquired with a tinge of respect.

"Yes. I couldn't believe Esther asked me to take her job with Levi," Dinah added. "I was so startled by this. She has to know the impression he makes."

"Esther probably knew nothing of Levi's words that day," *Mamm* suggested.

"She knew," Dinah responded, "because I told her about it myself, right after he made the remark in front of Abby."

"He might not have known she could hear him," *Grossmammi* suggested charitably.

"I don't think he cared," Dinah snorted. "Besides, she was right there, outside the Baumgartner *Haus* where the sermon was held that day."

"Maybe he didn't know Abby had come out of the *Haus*," Faith suggested.

"You may think he's innocent in all this, but I don't agree. He always looks at you as if he's just stepped in something nasty."

Her mother got up and crossed the kitchen to set her cup near the sink. Running a hand down Dinah's back, she said, "You love your sister and that's a good thing. *Geschwischder* should stand up for one another."

"But that doesn't mean you shouldn't take the job with Levi Becker," said her *Grossmammi*. "Abby herself told you to take the job and she's one to speak her mind. She'd have told you, if she didn't want you working with Levi."

"I still don't think I should do it."

"But didn't Esther tell you she'd tried everyone else?" Naomi queried. "At least, everyone Levi would work with."

"Yes, and how I made it on to that list, I don't know!"

"Levi won't work with an *Englischer*," her *Grossmammi* told her *Mamm*.

Wheeling around upon hearing this comment, Dinah said hotly, "There are other *Amische* who haven't been asked!"

"Esther said that you were her only hope," Faith reminded her. "I remember you telling me that. Either you work for Levi or she can't marry Jakob Moser."

"Has she asked Grace Schenkel or Amity Mellinger?" Naomi mentioned two of Dinah's closest friends.

"She has thought of them," Dinah said reluctantly. "Grace is already working with her sister and Amity has taken Becca's job, baking at the B&B. Besides, Esther said Levi doesn't want to work with Amity."

"Why?" Faith squinted as she asked the question.

"I don't know." Dinah waved a dismissive hand. "Something about Amity being too flighty and dizzy to be of any help."

The group of women fell silent, no one meeting any others' gaze.

Mamm cleared her throat. "Amity Mellinger is a lovely girl."

The others chimed in at the same time.

"She is."

"Yes, yes, that's true."

"She's very nice."

"But you know, Dinah," her *Grossmammi* said in a reasonable tone after a few minutes, "that Levi's not wrong about her."

Dinah's *Mamm* and sisters started chuckling. After a few minutes, she found herself joining them, the truth about Amity was irrefutable.

"I want Esther to be able to marry Jakob," Dinah said after a minute. "He's a good *Mann*."

"*Yah*," said her *Mamm*, her expression rueful and full of empathy. "Perhaps you should take Abigail at her word. Work the job."

"You can always quit," Naomi commented, "if Levi is a bad boss. If he's mean to you or unpleasant. I mean, he never was before, but if he is now, you can quit."

"You can," her *Grossmammi* agreed with a nod. "No one would blame you."

Dinah swallowed the protest that threatened at the back of her throat. Esther did deserve to marry and make her own life.

She sat, saying nothing, frustration rising up in her. Levi didn't deserve such a *gut* sister. Esther was a decent, kind girl to worry about her brother this way.

"Did Esther say Levi was a bad boss?" Naomi asked timidly.

"No," Dinah responded, "but she wouldn't have admitted that since she wants me to take the job."

"I suppose not," Faith put in, but we haven't heard anything like that."

"The *Ordnung* cautions us about passing judgment on our brothers," *Mamm* said.

"*Yah*." Dinah didn't know what to say to this. *Gott* knew that she'd had all kinds of judgmental thoughts about the *Mann* when she'd held a sobbing Abigail in her arms.

Still, it seemed that even her *familye* thought she ought to help Esther by working with Levi.

Esther drove her buggy at a fast pace the next morning, turning down several branching lanes. At least, it seemed fast to Dinah, nervously clinging to the buggy seat next to Esther. This might have been Dinah's anxiety at going to work for a kind of *Mann* who would hurt Abby. Levi's tall, muscular image sprang up before her eyes. He was a good-looking *Mann* with dark blond hair and blue eyes, but this didn't matter. He didn't seem like a person she wanted to help.

Her friend took another small lane that Dinah didn't know. She felt so bewildered by the various twists in the road that she could only hope she'd know how to make her way home, and she'd lived all her life in Fairfield County, Ohio.

"Come on!" Esther said eagerly when she came to a stop before a square, solid-looking building with a wide front window. "I told Levi we'd be there before he opened his doors this morning."

Feeling like there was lead in her shoes, Dinah wondered why she'd felt the need to go to the Becker *Haus* last night to tell her friend of her willingness to take the job. Thank goodness, Levi had still then been at his shop.

Not that she felt any more ready to face him this morning.

In no time, she found herself following her friend onto the wooden porch of a neat, compact building that held Levi's shop.

The thick February frost on the porch railings echoed Dinah's attitude at taking this step.

Eagerly pushing open the shop front door, Esther called out to her brother. "Levi! Levi!"

Dinah fidgeted with the strings of her *Kapp* and, in a moment, a dark blond head appeared at a curtain-covered doorway that seemed to open on the back of the shop.

She'd known Levi Becker all her life and been best friends with his *Schweschder* most of that. When he'd married and moved away, he had been a lighthearted *Mann* who teased and tormented her. Not the cold, unfriendly *Mann* who had returned to this part of the country.

"Welcome, Dinah Zook," Levi said, noting that his sister's best friend had grown into a woman while he was living in Millersburg. Light brown hair peeked from under her *Kapp*. He remembered her as being more blond. The blue eyes and fair skin were the same, though.

The expression on her face certainly wasn't that of someone eager for a job.

"*Hallo*," she responded, still with that somewhat defiant look on her face.

Her expression puzzled him, since Esther had spoken of Dinah's eagerness to find work. He randomly wondered if she still turned bright red when heated or embarrassed. She didn't seem embarrassed now. Levi scrutinized her face.

She actually looked mad.

"Well," Esther said brightly, gesturing around the room, "this is the stock of scooters and toys that Levi sells. And this, behind the counter, is the doorway to the back work area. Levi makes scooter and bicycle repairs."

"Oh." Dinah wandered over to a small display of wooden toys—cradles and pull toys in the shapes of various animals. "These are different."

"Yes," Esther responded in that same determined bright tone. "Levi sells some smaller toys that he makes in his spare time. Now, it'll be your job to enter sales into this ledger."

She pulled open a drawer behind the counter that held odds and ends, including a ledger book and pencils. "At the end of every week—and then at every month's end—you add up all the sales. We do inventory twice a year."

Silent as his sister chattered away, Levi thought again that he could handle this on his own—or find a more cheerful worker from somewhere. He'd come to prefer being alone. Of course, things got backed up sometimes…

Dinah's eyes really were a startlingly bright blue.

Suddenly, she asked him, her question challenging, "Do you want me to work here?"

"I do," Levi shot back without his usual consideration. "I do."

Dinah looked at him for a long moment and then said, as if she were still unsure of her own interest in the job, "Okay. What time tomorrow morning?"

CHAPTER TWO

"Don't you think the bicycles would look better propped against this wall?" Dinah asked in a sprightly voice that seemed a little forced. She continued in the same tight, chipper tone. "I think you're right to put the kick scooters in the rear here, by the counter. That way, shoppers pass everything else before they get to them."

Levi closed his eyes for a moment in exasperation. From the minute she walked in, Dinah had something to say. If she wasn't arranging bright orange field flowers to sit in a vase on the counter, she was engaged in a running, brittle commentary about everything in her morning.

"I'm so full! *Grossmammi* made the most delicious hootenanny pancakes." She paused to roll her eyes heavenwards as she rubbed her flat midsection.

"Usually, *Mamm* or Abby make breakfast and, even then, we get Friendship bread or Apea cake." Dinah gavc what sounded like a forced chuckle. "We never go hungry at our *Haus*. That's for sure."

The woman didn't seem to need a response from him, but just kept on with her chatter-talk. Levi had noted that she made sure she wasn't ever close to him, even if that required walking the long way around a room. Dinah was always more than an arm's length from him. She never looked at him directly, either, and he was also aware of a certain starch in her bearing, as if she didn't approve of him or was angry somehow?

They'd always been friendly before he moved away, so he wasn't sure why she seemed standoffish now.

Whatever the reason, having her here was disrupting his peace. His sister hadn't intruded on his quiet this way.

"Don't you think we should start a registry of all the addresses of your customers?" she asked in her bright tone. "I think that's best. Then we can send out notices when you get new toys."

Levi just looked at the wall in front of his work bench, not responding. The sunniness in her words didn't fit with the rigidity in her bearing. It was a puzzle.

He looked down at his work bench.

"Come sit by me," Grace Schenkel invited at the Sing two weeks later.

Huddling in her *Mamm*'s tufty gray sweater, loaned to protect her against a late February cold snap, Dinah acceded, lowering herself into one of the Augsberger's capacious chairs. "I was surprised to see Levi here," she commented to her friend, the words out of her mouth before she knew it.

She'd seen Levi at services all of her life, except for the years he'd lived away with his wife, and, heck, she worked with him. It was silly to now be so aware of him now.

"It was surprising," Grace agreed. "I think he only came to help the Augsberger boys with the volleyball standards.

"Those poles did look like they had big bases." Working with Levi was even more complex than she'd expected. He was quieter than she'd thought he'd be, which left her feeling unsure what was going through his head. Truthfully, every now and then he acted more like the *Buwe* she remembered growing up with than the unfriendly, standoffish *Mann* who'd made those ugly comments that were aimed at Abby.

But there was no mistaking that moment when he'd uttered his hurtful words.

Dinah shuddered, remembering how upset her sister had been. She'd already not liked Esther's brother after his unsmiling return, but his words had made her like him even less.

Across the room, a group of young *Menner* burst out laughing, drawing Dinah's gaze.

Saul Stutzman, Becca's new husband, was the oldest of the group of men and the one who'd made whatever comment that set the others to laughing. Levi sat with him, laughter softening a face that often had no expression now. With him sat her brother, Adam, Simon Groh and Joel Woomert—two young men of their congregation—and Jakob Moser, the *Mann* set to marry her friend, Esther.

The *Menne*r looked like they were having fun, Dinah observed. Even though Levi seemed to her like a cold, isolated *Mann,* he had friends. The fact was at odds with the way he'd treated her sister. Did his ugly side only come out with certain people? That couldn't be the truth. Everyone liked her sister.

Joel Woomert separated himself from the group, taking the path through the chairs that crossed in front of Dinah and Grace.

"Hallo, friends," he said smiling as he passed, headed toward dessert table.

"*Hallo*," the girls answered, Dinah's smile answering his.

"That apple pie you made was yummy," Dinah told Mary, turning back to her friend. "I've tasted your pies before, but this one was the best!"

"*Denki,"* Mary said with a smile, "I hope everyone thinks so."

The last statement was uttered with the serenity that was natural to her, but Dinah looked at her sideways. "If Aaron Rhoads gives you his attention, I don't think it'll be due to your apple pie."

"Aaron is known to have a sweet tooth," her friend responded placidly. "I don't think good pie could hurt."

"Neh," Dinah burst out laughing at that. "Do you plan to take up hunting and cornerball, too?"

"If need be." Mary gave her a twinkling smile.

"There are other *Menner*, you know, and several of them would love to drive you home and come take you for buggy rides."

"*Yah*, but Aaron just fits me best."

Dinah chuckled again. "I think it might be best if you let other *Menner* take you for buggy rides, just to check this out."

"Possibly. Why don't you accept buggy ride invitations? Not all young men are as fickle as Bart Altorfer."

Sobering, Dinah said, "I should ride out with other Menner. I guess I just don't care to risk finding out that they are like Bart. I guess no other young *Mann* has tempted me, so far."

"Seeing Bart with his new wife must be hard. It is difficult that they live in the area."

Dinah didn't like the compassion she saw in her friend's face. Mary meant only to be kind, she knew, but she recognized that pride made her hate this. It was sobering, really, because they were told to guard against pride of spirit.

"I thought I'd marry Bart," she said in a low voice.

"Until he learned that Tabitha Brandenberger had inherited a farm that just happens to be in this area," Mary commented in a tart tone.

Firming her lips, Dinah said in the same low tone, "Maybe *Gott* has better for me. We can't see down the road. *Gott* can and we must trust Him."

"*Gott* wouldn't have to look far to find better for you," Mary responded. "This is a good perspective for you to have. It means you're open to finding love with another."

Dinah shifted in her seat. "Perhaps, but I see no one now."

"You may not see him now," Mary said. "That doesn't mean he's not here."

"Maybe," Dinah responded doubtfully. Her gaze returned to the cluster of laughing men. Could she perhaps find herself in love with a *Mann* she already knew? Someone like Simon Groh or Joel Woomert? Somehow, it just seemed unlikely.

"Did you see Mark Hahn over there?" Mary asked.

Dinah sent a glance in the direction Mary had indicated with a bend of her head.

"*Neh*. I don't think I know him, though I may have seen him at the last meeting," she mused

"Yes, you do," her friend responded. "You just don't remember. He was several years ahead of us in school until his family moved away. He moved back here three or four months ago, but he only just started coming to church. Something about getting settled at the old Landis farm. I think I heard he was related to the Ausbergers. He's a widower with two boys."

Looking back at the tall, blond *Mann*, Dinah said, "He looks nice. I like his smile."

"My friend, Ada, who moved from Millersburg, not far from where Mark Hahn lived before, said he's been single for a year or so." Now Mary had swiveled to stare at the newcomer.

"Isn't Ada the girl who moved here to marry Hiram Kiefendorfer?" Dinah found herself staring as openly as was her friend.

"She is," Mary confirmed, "and with a name like that, he was lucky to find a *Frau.*"

Laughing in response to her friend's tart remark, Dinah said, "I need to go with my *Mamm* and sisters to meet Ada."

"If you're interested in Mark Hahn, you'd better get to know him, too. Maybe he's the 'better' *Gott* has for you," Mary said in a teasing voice. "Let's go get some dessert.

"You mean from the desserts over where Joel just went? Over where Mark Hahn is visiting with Simon Groh?" Dinah said, her lips twitching.

"How do you like moving back to Sugarcreek?" Huddling her coat around her to block out the cold, Dinah asked Mark Hahn later when he drove her home from the Sing that night,.

She still didn't know how this had happened so quickly. One minute she'd walked to the dessert table with Mary and the next, it seemed, she'd accepted Mark's invitation to let him drive her home. Her head was still spinning, but when he asked—and Mary gave her such a look—she'd found herself accepting.

The buggy horse trotted along the snowy roads lit by a full moon and before he answered her question, Mark Hahn asked, "Do I turn here?"

"Yes, the next left."

"I like it here very well," the tall dark-haired *Mann* said, his teeth gleaming in the moon's light as he sent her a smile. "Everyone has been so kind—well, most everyone."

The way he spoke, without resentment or heat, made Dinah ask, "Who hasn't been kind?"

The *Mann* beside her turned into her lane, the sides piled knee-high with snowbanks.

"I don't mean to sound ungrateful," Mark said quickly as the buggy horse trotted toward her *Haus*, "and we certainly aren't to talk about our brethren. The boys and I have found a great welcome here. Simon, my eldest who's about eight, was worried that he wouldn't find friends since school will let out in a few months until after the early fall harvest. That's why he went with the boys he met to this kick scooter shop."

A sudden mental image of Levi's unsmiling face popped into her head.

"Did he have a problem at the shop? I work there." She uttered the words in a wry tone.

"Oh! I shouldn't have said anything," the shadow of his wide brimmed hat turned toward her before he looked back at the road ahead.

"Hey," she responded, "maybe I was short with your son. Sometimes, the boys who come there get rowdy."

"*Neh*, it wasn't that…or you."

"It's the next drive on the right," she said.

"Denki." He directed the horse to turn in her drive, ice crunching under the wheels.

"Then what happened," she asked with the impetuousness her *Mamm* had counseled both her and Becca against.

"It was more than him being rowdy, too," Mark interjected quickly as he pulled the buggy to a stop.

"Well, tell me what happened," she urged. "It's not like I own the place. I'm just working there until my boss can find someone else. His sister is my friend and she got married and moved away recently."

Mark cleared his throat. "I don't suppose most businessmen would have done differently, at least, not *Englischers.*"

He'd turned back to address the horse's rump. "Not having much more than his allowance and naturally wanting a scooter like the other boys around here, Simon made an agreement with the shop owner—Becker—to work for him for several weeks. Simon was to earn a kick scooter then."

Dinah frowned in the murky light, not remembering any schoolboy hanging around to do Levi's bidding. "When was this?"

Mark shrugged. "Several months ago. This spring, Not long after we moved here. I bought a farm and it's run down, so I've had to give that all my attention for quite a while. The boys and I haven't even been going to church recently, we've been so busy. Of course, Simon is only eight. He couldn't do the heavy chores, so he worked at the scooter store for the number of weeks he was told would earn him a scooter—after he took care of our chickens and such—and he had a little money left from when we moved here. He threw that in, too. Well, Simon worked for this Becker, but when he'd done all that the *Mann* said he'd needed to do to get a scooter, your boss refused to give it to him. He said something about Simon needing to work several weeks more. I told my boy to quit. I promised to buy him a scooter myself, when I got a moment."

"That's horrible!" Dinah exclaimed.

The *Mann* beside her shrugged. "It's his shop, I suppose Becker can run it however he likes…"

"But this is wrong! And not Godly, at all."

"Perhaps not," Mark Hahn responded, "but I try not to judge."

"I cannot imagine how Levi could do such a thing," she said, her opinion of her boss sinking lower.

"Well, it's all over," Mark Hahn said, adding cheerfully. "Thank you for letting me drive you home."

"Here, Simon," Levi said to his friend several days later, "grab the other side of this and help me move it over there."

The two handily moved the wooden box to a raised area by the front window. "Now," Levi commented, "I can prop a kick scooter on it."

Aaron, Reuben and Simon had all taken the heavy blanket of fog on the ground to enjoy gathering in Levi's shop that day.

"He's a good beast of burden," Aaron said of their friend, his lip quivering, "even if he's not popular with *Maedels*."

Simon only responded with a goofy smile, scratching his belly, as he straightened from having helped Levi.

Everyone knew that he was to inherit his uncle's farm and would, when Simon was ready to seriously start looking, have no difficulty finding a wife.

As the group's chuckles subsided, Reuben ventured to protest. "Simon is no more a beast of burden than we all are, at one time or another."

With the heavy blanket of fog on the ground, Levi's shop was empty of customers. It wasn't to be expected that any of the children, that often dragged their parents into the shop, could be spared from tending farm animals on such a cold, rainy day.

Listening to the back and forth of his friend's cheerful conversation, Levi's mind again returned to having had a recent visit from their bishop.

He needed to marry again, the bishop had said. Levi had mourned long enough, the cleric had declared.

How long is long enough, Gott? Why do I feel as if there's still a hole in my chest?

"Oh, *Neh*, my friend!" Simon shouted in response to something Aaron had said.

Smiling at the easy comradery that flowed all around him, Levi shifted a toy on the counter to lean closer. His friendships here had kept him sane in the months since Anna and the baby died. Moving home had been the right action to take.

"I hear that Aaron's going for drives with a particular girl now," Reuben inserted with a sly smile.

Pulling his mouth down in a serious manner, Simon said in a deep voice, "We are not to be chattering about our neighbors. What may have been said to you, my friend, should not be passed on."

Not abashed at all, Aaron said irreverently, "Especially, in front of a future bishop!"

The group broke into laughter, with Levi saying after a moment, "Stop giving Reuben a hard time. Don't you all want to say you have been friends, all this long time, with a bishop?"

Still chuckling, Reuben said, "Do not talk of future honors. We none of us know what *Gott* has for us in the days ahead."

"Then what shall we talk about?" Simon asked, a twinkle in his eyes. "*Maedels*? I believe Aaron is consistently walking out with that girl we will not name—as we dare not lead him into bragging about his connection. Do you have any observations to add, Reuben? Or you, Levi?"

"What can we say?" Levi retorted, the bishop's admonition on his mind.

"I am not suggesting we pass judgment on our neighbors," Aaron responded. "Just that we can comment on that which we've noticed."

"Mary Yost seems always to have a sister or brother at her side," Simon commented, his expression ridiculously innocent. "I had thought to drive her home, after the last Sing, but I can only fit two in my buggy."

"Dinah Zook is always chattering." The observation was out of Levi's mouth before he knew it, landing in their conversation just as the laughter after Reuben's words had settled.

"Doesn't she now work with you?" Aaron asked, his question offered into the small silence that had fallen after Levi's words.

"Yah." All eyes on him, he wished he'd just kept his mouth shut. "She's worked at the shop only a short time, but she's always offering ideas and saying things, as if she can't stand silence."

"What a horrible quality," Simon said, the twinkle back in his gaze.

"Well, it can be annoying," Levi countered.

"What conversations do you have with her?"

Not sure how to respond to Reuben's question, Levi hesitated.

"Yes," Aaron agreed, a small wrinkle appearing between his brows. "Perhaps, she's just trying to make conversation with you."

"Dinah Zook is a nice girl," Simon inserted, as if this was under discussion. "She's a heck of a good softball pitcher, too."

"Of course, you would say that," Levi shot back. "She pitched for your team in that softball game."

"She did," Simon agreed, satisfaction in his words.

"The trouble is, that even though she's always what a good employee should be…" Levi searched for the words to convey what troubled him, "I can't but think she's angry with me. Specifically, with me. I've heard her to talk to several customers, of different ages, and she's very friendly when she speaks to them."

"But not to you?" Reuben had a worried look on his face.

"Not to me. Mind you, she's not ugly or unkind. Her suggestions for the shop may not fit exactly with mine, but they seem sincere. I just can't ignore that—underneath—she's angry with me."

The group fell silent, seeming to consider Levi's quandary, when Aaron spoke up, obviously picking his words carefully. "It might have—something to do with—"

"With what?" Levi asked irritably. The girl Aaron had been driving with recently was Mary Reese, a close friend of Dinah's.

"With what you said about Gabe Eichelberger having died without *Kinder,*" Aaron rushed into speech. "Dinah's sister, Abigail, was his *Frau*."

"What-what did I say?" Levi's mind shuffled through his sometimes garbled memory. "Was it something I said shortly after I moved back here?"

"You had moved back a while before that I think." Aaron looked uncomfortable.

"Well, what did I say?" Levi knew he sounded as irritable as he felt. Anna's and the baby's deaths didn't occupy nightly dreams anymore, but he still didn't like thinking about his loss.

Aaron cleared his throat, then said manfully, "Like I said, you made comments about Abigail's husband having died without *Kinder*."

"And?" Levi asked irritably. "It's the truth. They didn't have children."

With visibly increasing discomfort, Aaron said, "No, and Abigail Eichelberger feels badly about this. At least, that's what her sisters say, and you made the comment about Gabe Eichelberger having died childless where Abby could hear you. Dinah's mad at you for causing her sister distress."

"I didn't know Abigail was listening!" Levi countered in a defensive voice. "I certainly didn't say anything to her face."

"Apparently," Aaron said heavily, "she overheard you."

'I don't see how that's my fault. I didn't mean her any criticism, but it's just a reality that Gabe died without children."

He felt defensive and a little appalled that he'd said anything. Still, not for one solid moment could any of these men know the pain of having lost both his wife and child, Levi thought, his mouth closing firmly over the words that might sound accusatory. He'd moved on…enough to listen calmly to the bishop's marriage recommendation, but he still felt his loss.

What he needed was a woman to marry that he could tolerate—but who he didn't love passionately. He just didn't know where to find such a creature.

"Well, that's the reason Dinah may seem—may seem a little unfriendly," Aaron finished, as one who wanted out of the conversation.

"Oh. Okay." Levi knew he might sound ungracious, but laying out all of what had been going on with him back then would be like opening his skin for all his organs to be seen. He just didn't know how to do it.

"Well, anyone for a ball game in the fog?" Reuben asked with cheer that seemed a little forced.

The other men chuckled.

Simon propped his feet comfortably on the rail that ran around the wood stove. "I have chores at home that I probably should do."

"You seem highly motivated to get to them," Levi commented, glad the focus was no longer on him and Dinah.

"Oh, I am. I am," Simon assured him. "There are always repairs to the buggy harness and wood to chop."

Levi waited a moment before his friend continued.

"There's always wood to chop," Simon volunteered, raising his empty coffee mug with a smile "It's not going anywhere."

Dinah tromped up the back porch stairs, balancing the full laundry basket against her hip. As she pulled the kitchen door open, she glanced over at the lines strung between two poles. An empty clothesline always gave her satisfaction.

Her arms full of the basket filled with clothes still chill with the cold snap, she let the door bang shut behind her.

The kitchen was unusually silent, only Abby at the stove, stirring a pot of something.

"I've got it all in," Dinah announced with satisfaction. "Let the rain come now! Maybe it will wash away the fog."

As Dinah set the basket into a kitchen chair, she caught the faint sound of a sniffle at the stove.

Swiftly turning, she gazed at her sister, noting the hunched shoulders.

"Abigail?" She moved to lay a hand on her sister's back. "*Schweschder?* Are you crying?"

"No," responded her sister in a hard, taut voice, "Of course, not."

Dinah continued to study her, noting the swift wiping of one cheek. "You are crying."

"*Neh!*" Abby was more emphatic this time.

Turning toward Dinah, she said, "We all have our times, sister. Do you not have days that you're low? Times that—for no clear reason—you think about all the hard times in your life?"

In the flash of an instant, Dinah saw again Bart Altorfer standing in front of her, announcing that, instead of marrying her, he was instead marrying the wealthy Tabitha Brandenberger. Never mind that *Gott* had instructed them to choose riches in Heaven.

Her sister standing, waiting for an answer, Dinah admitted, "Yes, I have those moments."

"Of course, you do." Abby turned back to the stove. "We all do."

Shifting back another chair at the table, Dinah sat down. "Why are you having this now? Is there a reason?"

If her working for Levi Becker caused any distress to her sister, Dinah would march in there tomorrow and quit. All that Mark Hahn told her made her want to quit, anyway.

Oddly, after this short time of working in his shop, it would be strange not to see Levi's face every day, but she couldn't cause Abby pain and she certainly didn't want to work for a *Mann* who cheated *Youngies*.

Quitting would also be a relief in some murky way.

"I suppose," Abby admitted to the pot she'd been stirring, "that it's hard seeing Becca so happy with Saul."

"Becca and Saul?" Dinah knew she probably sounded as astonished as she was.

"*Yah*." Abby sounded disgusted with herself as she shifted the pot off the burner and turned the flame off. "They are so happy together. Saul's harder to read, but I don't think I've ever seen Becca this happy."

Baffled still, Dinah continued to search Abby's face.

Her sister came to sit with her at the table.

"Gabe and I were that happy once."

Her face crumpled before Dinah's astonished gaze. Reaching out impulsively, she grabbed Abby's hand. Her *Schweschder* rarely showed strong emotion and seeing her cry twice in such a short time was unsettling. It was just part of Abigail's makeup that she seemed level. Most of the time.

"Yes, you and Gabe were always happy."

"We were," Abby agreed in a hard voice, "until he died. That was bad enough, but to die with no *Kinder*. I know *Gott* sends children as a blessing to those who deserve this, but Gabe was a kind and good *Mann*. I know, too, that the fault of having no children was mine."

She got up and began shaking out a sheet from the chilly basket of laundry.

Still startled by the entire moment, Dinah just swallowed and stared at her. "I'll quit working with that Levi Becker!"

"Neh. It's all right." Abby used that hard, brisk voice again as she folded the sheet, "these moments don't last long. I will just attend to the tasks of the day."

Dinah felt just awful.

"It's all right, sister," Abigail said with a smile after a moment. "I'm all right."

Dinah looked at Abby through tears that had suddenly flooded her eyes, stricken and feeling even worse about working for Levi.

CHAPTER THREE

Watching her younger sister, several days later, Dinah tried to braid the columns of bread dough, on the counter in front of her, the same way as Becca.

The farm kitchen was warm and homey, the scent of fresh bread, from Becca's earlier batch, permeating every part of the room.

"It's good," Becca giggled. "Being married is good."

"You're just saying that because you're crazy for Saul," their friend Amity teased with a chuckle. Sitting across from Dinah, she seemed to be having the same difficulty with the bread dough as was Dinah.

Sitting next to Becca, their friend Amity laughingly agreed, while Becca blushfully protested.

The sisters and friends were in the Zook's cheerful kitchen, the windows open to release the heat from the oven into the cool air.

"You are all just silly *Maedels*," their *Grossmammie* Ruth said with a chuckle. "What do any of you know about spending your lives with a Mann?"

"*Grossmammi* is right," Becca interjected. "I've only been married a short time, but it's been long enough for me to realize that being married means learning your whole life. Saul helps me see when I'm being short-sited and I help soften him, I think. We all have our places."

Amity flopped her bread dough in the pan. "I'm tired of learning. It tires me out!"

Sympathetic laughter surfaced from several in the room, as the chuckles drifted away,

Grossmammi Rose said, "It is tiring when you're in it alone. I've felt this since *Grossdaddi* passed."

"*Yah,*" agreed Becca. "Everything is better…easier, when shared. It seems all burdens are carried by the two of you, as a team pulls a plow."

Dinah pondered for a minute. She'd like to feel that way about a *Mann,* like they were together in everything.

"I saw Mary driving out with Aaron Rhoads," Grace announced, smiling.

"He only saw I had an armful of groceries and offered me a ride," Mary said, flushing.

"And what of Dinah's brother, Adam?" teased Grace, "Won't he feel sad that you're driving out with another *Buwe*?"

"Now, girls," *Grossmammi* interjected before a red-faced Mary answered, "let us not speak of others, but leave their business to them and to *Gott*."

"Of course," Grace responded, looking chastened.

"Yes, let's do that." Mary seemed both relieved and triumphant, making a face at Grace.

"You came here for a baking lesson," Becca reminded them, her prim tone leavened by the impudent grin on her face.

Dinah stood for a moment, thinking about *Grossmammi's* words. She'd heard this same thing throughout her life. She'd also been taught not to judge others or to hold grudges, although she didn't know what to do in the face of Mark Hahn's information. Her parents had always directed the siblings to try to emulate *Gott* in forgiving.

She drew a deep breath. It all seemed so different when Abby's hurt came to mind, too, and unfriendly Levi Becker's chilly expression rose up before her mind's eye. He was so different than the laughing *Mann* she remembered. Not that this mattered much. He was now what he was.

"Here," her sister showed up at Dinah's elbow, "let me show you." Beneath Becca's deft fingers, the loaf of bread took on something looking like a braid of dough.

Becca squeezed her shoulders in a tight hug. "Don't worry, sister. My first attempts at bread were really dismal."

"Maybe," Dinah responded, glumly, "but this isn't my first attempt. Why I'm older than you. I should have learned how to make a simple loaf of bread!"

"This isn't a simple loaf of bread," Becca said in a scolding voice. "Just keep at it and you'll learn."

Dinah didn't believe for an instant that she'd ever be as good a baker as Becca. She might learn to braid bread, but she didn't have the love of baking that Becca did.

Later, after their friends left, she trailed out to the kitchen garden that looked in late March about as bleak as she felt. Wisps of dry leaves fluttered in the fencing around the plot of land and rich brown dirt rows lay dormant in the cold.

Dinah hated her dilemma. She was working for a *Mann* who represented all the things she disliked, but she didn't have another job, so she had to make the best of it. She could, however, confront him about his cruel actions. At least, she could do that.

The next morning, Levi counted again the cash in the register, looking up when he heard a knock on the locked shop door.

His stomach tightened when he saw the dark shape through the glass door. He hurried to the door to let the bishop in from the cold. Even though February was now leading into March, the air had turned colder in the night.

"*Goedemorgen,* Levi," Bishop Kolb said, going to the wood stove to warm his hands. "The air is cold this morning. As if spring hadn't come, at all?"

"Perhaps you'd like to come to the back room to sit a while?" Despite his dislike of the subject he knew the bishop had come to discuss, he wanted to be gracious to the *Mann*. Levi had nothing against Bishop Kolb. He served the community well.

"Ach! The wind is cold!" The older man warmed his hands by the stove, the grate glowing bright with the embers inside warming the room.

Levi held the curtain back, gesturing to the bishop to follow him. When Bishop Kolb followed him to the chairs beside the stove in the back room, Levi sat down on the outer edge of the wooden seat, steeling himself for the subject he knew was at hand.

"Well," the bishop started, rubbing his hands together again in front of these coals, "have you given thought to the matter I spoke to you about?"

His bushy brows rose with the question.

"I have." Levi's spine straightened more.

"*Gut*, good," Bishop Kolb smiled as if he'd given the right answer. "You know that, in this, *Gott* has your best interests, as do all the bishops in the area,"

Levi's mouth felt dry and he suddenly couldn't find words. He certainly couldn't respond to this in the negative. As his speech seemed to have abandoned him, Levi nodded.

"It is, of course," Bishop Kolb went on, "that you will find happiness, and the answer to your prayers, in a *Maedel* in this area."

Levi knew he couldn't tell the Bishop that he had no desire to marry again, no ability to lay himself open again to feelings that had almost stolen his life when Anna had died. No *Amishe* could say that *Gott* preferred them to live alone. All knew that each was to face life with a marital partner at their side. How else would they beget the *Kinder* that were *Gott's* gift?

All his life he'd looked forward to being the *Daed* of a handful of children, to hold their small hands in his and listen to their high voices calling out to him.

For the flash of a moment, he thought of poor, dead Grace, the little girl who had been taken before she'd even drawn a breath. How would her voice have sounded?

"There are several *Maedels* in this area that aren't involved with other *Menner,*" the bishop said.

Levi swallowed. Despite his belief that *Gott* didn't want him to live alone, everything in Levi rebelled at the thought of putting himself out there again. He couldn't imagine loving another woman as he'd loved Anna.

The bishop droned on, saying words that Levi couldn't dispute. All he kept thinking was he'd never be able to risk that damage again.

Later, Levi closed the shop door behind the bishop, making sure to do this quietly, despite his internal turmoil. He knew he should marry again. It wasn't necessary for the bishop to keep reminding him. He knew God's words that *Mann* needed a helpmate by his side.

He'd be married by now, but Levi hadn't been able to choose a *Maedel.* How could he marry a woman who expected a fully-open husband? Expected to be cherished and taken as a partner in every aspect of his life?

He wasn't going to again lay out his heart. He couldn't. That organ had been ripped out of him when Anna and the *Boppli* died. He didn't have another heart to give a woman.

Getting ready to open the shop later, Levi replaced the pencil in the counter drawer after marking another tick on the page. He liked to keep the inventory updated. He hated to admit it, but Dinah's help in the shop made his workload lighter. She had made several changes in how he'd set everything up. This irritated him and he hated that he valued anything about her, at all. He got himself in trouble when he cared.

"We should move the small wooden toys to the front, beside the register," Dinah commented several hours later.

Levi looked at her solemnly without comment.

"That way," she continued, forcing herself to speak pleasantly, "your buyers will see the toys when they're checking out and make impulse buys."

Levi cleared his throat, drawing Dinah's gaze to him. "I don't wish to trick children into buying what they don't need."

"Of course, not," she shot back angrily, "but you have said that the wooden toys are well made. You make them yourself!"

He studied her face without comment.

"You know you have." Sometimes the *Mann* really irritated her!

"I must admit," Levi finally said in a grudging tone, "that you've made some good changes to the shop. Things I wouldn't have thought of."

"*Denki*," Dinah said, letting out a calmer breath.

"Despite my initial concerns," he observed slowly, "most of the time, we work well together."

She looked at him, eyeing him in suspicious disbelief.

"As a matter of fact," Levi said slowly, "we make a good team."

The strange note in his voice made her stare at him. She couldn't find a reply.

Levi stared at Dinah later that day, as she swept the floor in the back room. He felt stunned, a startling idea ricocheting around in his brain. He didn't love this *Maedel*. He felt nothing for Dinah Zook…but she was a good worker. She seemed to fit right in with his shop.

Yah, their interaction was always tinged with her faint hostility, but he didn't mind her astringent quality. It kept everything well defined…and clear. There was nothing of the heart in this.

She might be the answer to his dilemma. Maybe. He had to think about it.

As the bishop kept reminding him, he needed to marry again and Levi was resolute that he would not risk his heart this time.

It seemed clear to him that he needed a *Frau* he didn't love, but who he respected. A woman with whom to fulfill *Gott's* direction. Someone with whom to have children and raise a family. Someone who didn't drive him crazy.

Maybe Dinah did drive him crazy sometimes, but overall, the positives of this plan outweighed the bad. He needed to think about this.

Two days later, Dinah was washing down the wide front shop windows. The shop door was propped open to let in the breeze and Levi tinkered with the wheels of a kick scooter that rested on the shop's front counter.

She looked up from her task to find that his gaze rested on her. Dinah paused in scrubbing at a small, grubby handprint on the glass.

"What?"

His gaze was usually dark, but this seemed more intent. "You have been of help here."

Dinah looked back at him, saying with some suspicion, "Thanks…."

"I told Esther that I didn't need help here, but you've made some *gut* suggestions." Despite his complimentary words, Levi didn't smile.

She paused a moment before responding, "I appreciate you saying that."

Levi nodded. "I think we should get married."

Wondering for a second if she'd heard him right, she blinked.

"We are neither of us *Youngies* and we can both work here while building a family." He stopped, still looking at her, his hands paused in his work.

Not even answering the insult about her age that was implied in his words, Dinah let her window washing rag drop to the floor.

"I think we should get married," he repeated.

Words crowding onto her tongue, she took a breath to hold them back.

Her cheeks feelingly flushed with her indignation, Dinah bent to her bucket before she stood and started washing the window again.

"Well?"

His inquiry was tinged with impatience.

"I'm grateful for your offer," she managed after a pause, "but I don't think we would suit."

Dinah sent him a forced smile before bending to dip her rag in the bucket, outraged and relieved that she'd so politely responded.

"Wouldn't suit?" Levi stared at her, seeming all unaware. "Oh, I'm sorry. Are you courting with someone else? I should have asked. I saw Joel Woomert talking to you at the Sing and Bart—it was Bart?—and you used to spend a lot of time together when you were *Youngies.*"

Her wet rag dropped into the bucket as Dinah stiffened, glaring at him as she said, "No, I'm not courting with someone else! You think that is the only reason I wouldn't accept your offer?"

She couldn't believe that he looked at her, uncomprehending.

Levi felt his face heat as they faced off. "What are you talking about?"

He knew, of course. Even if Aaron hadn't said anything about it, Levi now remembered his bitter remark It had been a bad day following a bad night and he'd spoken out of his loss. If truth be told, he'd hoped Dinah's practical side would lead her not to bring up the subject.

Knowing his cheeks were as red as hers had grown, he quickly said, "I'm sorry. Of course, you're probably courting with another *Mann.* I haven't heard a lot of the news as I've been working on getting the shop started since having moved home. I apologize."

Dinah gasped in startled anger.

"That is really why you think I'm rejecting your proposal? Because I'm with another *Mann*? Of course, why else would your offer be rejected? Are you completely without conscience?" she demanded. "How could you act as you have and still wonder at my refusal?"

Levi's expression became rigid. "I don't believe I have no conscience. You're refusing me absolutely? And not because of another *Mann*? Have you some concept of marriage being only right between those in love?"

The last two words were said with scorn.

"*Neh*," she said, "others may do what they think best, but, even if I wanted such a practical, business union like that, I would never marry a *Mann* whose cruel words hurt my sister or who treated Mark Hahn's son so badly."

"Mark Hahn?" Completely baffled at her words, he could do no more than repeat the name. "What about Mark Hahn?"

"I am amazed that you look so innocent after trying to cheat the boy!"

"What are you talking about?" Levi knew he sounded irritable. "I let the *Buwe* pay for a scooter by working off the debt. That's all. How is that cheating him?"

She appeared to have forgotten the windows and the bucket of water as she squared up to him. "You claim to have given him a kick scooter?!"

"No! I told you. He worked it off." He tried to level his tone. "He worked and then I gave him a scooter.'

"That's not what Mark said!"

"Oh, yes. I've been so mean to Mark Hahn. He and I have a rocky past. It must have colored what he said." Containing his contempt was very hard, but Levi reflected on *Gott* turning the other cheek. Doing so didn't help much.

"And what you said about my sister?"

"I understand that your sister overheard a comment I made to a friend. I said nothing to her and nothing that was not true," he defended. "Nothing your sister did not know."

"Abby was heartbroken!" Dinah exclaimed. "I've never seen her cry like that. Even when Gabe died, she held herself together. How could you be so cruel?"

Although he was more distressed by her response than he had thought he'd be, Levi grappled to pull together a dignified reply.

He didn't want to lose her help with his shop. Yes, that was it. That was what drove this bad feeling in his stomach.

"Very well, *Maedel,*" he said stiffly after a moment. "You have given me your answer. I simply laid out a path that we could take. Think no more of it. I assure you that I will not trouble you with this again. We will work together as before."

Feeling this needed to be conveyed and reminding himself that she was the best worker he'd ever had, Levi stuck out his hand. "I want you to work here, even though you rejected my suggestion."

For a long minute, Dinah stared at his hand, as if she'd be taking a hot coal into her palm if she took it.

He watched her, indecision written across her face. Finally, after several minutes, she stretched out her hand and pressed it quickly against his.

In that rushed moment—the press of her warm hand against his—Levi knew danger. He realized he cared what Dinah Zook thought. He cared.

This would never do.

CHAPTER FOUR

"Adam?" Dinah paused that evening, perched on the front porch steps.

Her elder brother looked up from cleaning the buggy horse harness. "What?"

"How do you know when someone is telling you the truth?" Mark Hahn had an open face and an honest manner. It did not seem that he wasn't being honest in his story.

Adam took a moment to answer, as if he was considering her question. "I guess I'd take into account whether he has lied to me before."

"What if he was new to you? Like if you'd just met him?" She didn't know why she was asking. What she knew of Levi Becker didn't really leave her with much doubt. His character seemed clear.

"That's trickier," Adam went back to his work. "In that case, I'd look at what the newcomer said and did. Does he seem kind to others?"

"Yes," Dinah interjected.

Adam went on "Does he talk kindly of others? Does he do what he says? That sort of thing."

She hesitated. As far as she knew Mark did what he said. Looking at what she knew of him, he was very likely telling the truth about the interaction between Levi and Mark's son.

Dinah came to work a few minutes late the next morning, having walked more slowly through the spring morning. Thank *Gott*, the weather had warmed and here and there blossoms bloomed. Although the rain had brought fog, it also helped growing things.

Following the lanes towards Levi's shop, shaded by loblolly pine and paw paw trees, she brooded over the previous day's conversation.

He'd asked her to marry him!!

Just that reality floored her.

Seen in just a business light, many would say she should have accepted his proposal. She wasn't a *Youngie* anymore, as he'd pointed out. Many *Maedels* were *Mamms* by the age of 23. Dinah's mouth quirking up on one side, she swished the stick she carried though the long grass, dotted with white trillium flowers, at the lane's edge.

Thankfully, her *Eldre* had never pushed her to wed.

Levi's shop was prosperous. There was no other scooter shop for miles around, however. Having no competition, the shop did pretty well. The shop was always full of kids, mostly boys.

One of five siblings, Levi had four sisters. As he was in the middle and was the only *Buwe*, it was still unlikely that his *Eldre* would have been able to help him purchase a farm. His family wasn't wealthy, but Levi had found his own path.

Stopping to jerk loose a stalk of Virginia bluebell, she scowled at the dangling blue buds. Even if he hadn't committed the sin of making her stoic sister cry, he was cold to new acquaintances and stared with a chilly expression when he didn't approve of her actions. Dinah knew, because she'd been on the receiving end of a few of those cold glances.

So different than Esther's brother had been before!

And then he'd proposed! If you could call it that. Never once had he even said he liked her, just that they worked well together.

Well, given his resistance to some of her ideas, Dinah was surprised to hear even that.

Dinah left the lane, following a short cut through a cool wooded path to the shop. Stopping at the clearing that circled Levi's shop, she exhaled a deep breath before going inside.

The situation should be awkward after her last conversation with Levi. He certainly wasn't the only *Mann* in her life. She might not be courting with any certain *Mann* yet, but that didn't mean she had no admirers.

Later that afternoon, Dinah stood behind the counter at Levi's shop, musing over how quickly everything between them had returned to what it had been before. At least, it seemed that way. She thought that—given the option—she'd never have spoken to him again, but theirs was too small a community for that.

The shop front door was propped open now, as was the back, allowing the cool spring air to circulate. The earthy smell of a neighboring farmer's newly mown field next door mingled with the scent from a cluster of daffodils Dinah had found on her walk to work this morning. They occupied a dusty jar on the counter, their bright yellow heads nodding in the breeze rustling through the shop.

It seemed strange to her that matters between her and Levi should be so matter-of-fact after they'd had such a heated exchange. It wasn't like she'd forgiven him and he'd not even asked for forgiveness. The *Bisskatz.*

He was outside now, surrounded by boys as was often the case, she noted. To her surprise, Levi seemed like a different *Mann* when he was with his young customers. They came to show him their newly-acquired tricks on their kick scooters and just to hang out with friends.

Curious now at what kept him longer outside, Dinah skirted the counter and went to the glass front door.

At first, all she saw was a group of several kids—even a young girl—surrounding the taller Levi, who stood bare-headed, his hat obviously discarded.

Then as the milling bunch around him shifted, Dinah saw young Micah Spanky, who'd apparently brought in his corn hole board, demonstrating this for Levi.

Corn hole wasn't an exotic game for members of their community, but Levi had seemingly missed out on playing the game and was…from the scene in front of her, now playing the game with the smaller Micah.

Straining her ears, her suspicion that Levi was playing the game to beat the *Buwe* was corrected. As Micah was instructing the taller *Mann*, Levi bent down with an attentive expression on his face.

He didn't look cool or disinterested now.

Dinah's mouth quirked up on one side. The boy was clearly enjoying his role.

"No, no, underhand! Like this Mister Becker."

"I can't quite get the hang of it, Micah. Show me again."

Micah sent another bean bag, lofted toward the corn hole board. When it landed square in the middle hole, her boss groaned, his hand lifted to cover his face.

She drew nearer, leaning against the front door jamb. From the sounds of it, Levi was taking Micah's instructions, actually letting the boy teach him to play.

Not knowing how to take this laughing, teasing version of Levi, Dinah watched him, caught up in the gentle interplay of the two. The children crowded around them were clearly cheering for Micah.

Her ears pricking up, she heard one of the kids call another boy, Simon.

Simon Hahn? This child seemed to have no hard feelings with Levi.

When Levi had thrown bean bag after bean bag—often with Micah offering a severe commentary—her boss turned suddenly toward the door.

So suddenly that, Dinah, raptly caught up in the scene, had to scramble away from the door, adjusting her expression and pretending to arrange a toy display near the shop entrance.

And Simon Hahn was here? Maybe his father hadn't been telling the truth, after all.

The Levi that played with the children surely seemed very different than the cold, unfriendly *Mann* who'd asked her to marry him.

The next afternoon, Levi was in the middle of adjusting a kick scooter on the store counter when Amity Mellinger, a friend of Dinah's trailed her four-year-old brother into the shop. As Jakob Mellinger ran to play with the small wooden toys Levi had made, Amity went to talk with Dinah, who was also behind the counter, several feet from Levi.

"I saw you driving out with Ezekiel Bassler," Amity teased. "What are your intentions there?"

"I have no intentions," Dinah returned calmly. "Ezekiel is like a brother to me and he's good friends with Adam."

Amity hoisted herself to sit on the counter near Dinah. "Since when has that stopped anyone from courting with a *Mann*? Love happens where it happens."

Levi couldn't help himself, shamelessly listening to the interchange.

Dinah snorted. "Well, it hasn't happened with Zeke, so don't get excited."

"You were driving out with him," Amity responded with a laugh.

"It was purely a convenience," Dinah said. "I had a lot of bundles, as I'd gone shopping, and he happened along with a buggy."

Slipping off the counter, Amity casually looked at the kick scooter that Levi had placed near the register. "That's too bad. Ezekiel Baughman is an elder son and he works with his father on the family farm. He'll probably take over the farm and that's not nothing. He also has nice manners."

"What are you," Dinah retorted, "my mother? You have nothing but marriage on your mind. It's all that time you're spending with Aaron Rhoads."

His mouth kicking up on one side, Levi shot a side look at the girls, continuing to bend over the scooter.

In his quick glance, he saw that Amity had taken on a pious expression that, at the same time, managed to look self-satisfied.

The girl said, "I don't know what you mean. Marriage is no more important to me than it is to any other *Maedel*."

Snorting, Dinah moved over to bend down next to Amity's young brother. "Isn't that wooden horse amazing?"

"*Yah*!" Jakob replied with visible enthusiasm. He lifted the horse up and down, making clip-clop sounds. "I'd name him Ash."

Having come over to stand next to Jakob, Amity said in a teasing voice, "But we already have a horse named Ash! You know, the horse that pulls our buggy?"

"I know," her brother responded in his high-pitched, youthful voice. "I just like that name."

Patting the small boy's back, Dinah said, "I think Ash is a good name."

After her friend had left—the small Jakob trailing behind Amity—Dinah stood straightening a toy arrangement on a wide table in front of the counter when Levi came from behind the counter. Her side vision informed her that her boss had leaned casually against the counter.

Having taken off his jacket, his sleeves were rolled up, revealing a sprinkle of dark hair on his lower arms.

Dinah swallowed and sternly refocused her attention on the toys in front of her. It was ridiculous to be so aware of him now. So what if he had proposed? He really meant nothing of it. Nothing more than a business proposition. They worked side by side daily.

Amity's remarks about her driving out with Ezekiel had probably raised Dinah's sensitivity.

"It's almost time to close," Levi announced suddenly. He straightened from the counter and, before she knew it, had grabbed Dinah's hand. "I need to go by the general store. Come with me."

"What?" This was new. "Do you need to get things for the store?"

Not used to the feel of Levi's hand in hers, she felt a tingle run up her arm.

She couldn't imagine what might have been needed there as she'd gotten into the routine habit of leaving lists of needed supplies. Somehow, these items all materialized.

"The store," he repeated. "Go with me."

"Okay," she managed as he dragged her behind him to shut the shop's front door.

Twenty minutes later, Levi pulled his buggy into a drive that made Dinah's mouth drop open. "What are we doing here?"

"This is the first night of the county fair," he informed her.

"I know, but this is an *Englischer* fair," she said in what she knew was a tone that reflected her surprise.

"Most of it," Levi agreed, tying the buggy reins to the bar that ran across the box, "but several of our *Fraus* are running the food booths. I felt hungry."

"Okaaayyy," she said again, not resisting when he gestured her to slide across the seat. Then—in a totally unexpected move—he grabbed her by the waist and lifted her down, placing her on ground next to him. Startled, Dinah drew in another deep breath and then stopped herself as the clean, soap scent of him filled her lungs. Before she knew it, he'd matter-of-factly reached into the buggy for his jacket while she stood waiting next to him, docile as a lamb.

Dinah hardly recognized herself. She couldn't remember the last time this description fit her. He might be a *Mann* who cheated small boys—although Simon Hahn's demeanor said otherwise—and said mean things within her *Schweschder's* hearing.

This lamb-like behavior wasn't at all like her and Dinah could only attribute her compliance to the shock of his nearness. Sure, she worked beside the *Mann* every day, but never had she had this kind of contact with him.

It…unsettled her.

There were several buggies parked near them under the trees as she stood, waiting again as he fetched a bucket of water for his buggy horse.

Dinah knew she shouldn't be here like this. Certainly, should be anywhere with Levi, but she couldn't exactly come up with a reason that it was unwise. Caught in her indecision, she waited next to the horse, wavering.

"Come on," he said, grabbing her hand for the second time ever.

It crossed her mind that she might be dreaming, although she had no idea why she'd dream this.

After reaching and walking along the fair's center aisle, Levi dropped her hand.

Dinah said nothing, feeling like a fool for even being here. She didn't even like him and *Englischer* county fairs weren't for her. Ironically, a number of *Amische* passed them as they walked down the aisle.

"The *Fraus'* food booth is right over there," Levi commented, leading the way.

Starting to follow him, she then froze, stopping in her steps.

Not six feet away from her was Bart Altorfer and her past opened up at the brutal sight.

Her breath locking in her chest, Dinah couldn't move forward. She'd thought, at one time, that she'd marry Bart.

Gott must have other plans for her, as her sister had pointed out, but never had she been more wrong about a *Mann.*

Dinah blinked.

Since they worshipped at the same *Gmay*, she hadn't been able to avoid seeing Bart and his new wife, Tabitha, but she'd tried not to be within talking distance of the *Mann* who she'd thought to marry. Before he'd dumped her and married the wealthy Tabitha.

By now several feet ahead, Levi looked back, walking to where she stood.

Seeing Tabitha Altorfer finally—next to the perfidious Bart—leaning over the counter at the pastry booth, Dinah gasped in a breath. She saw them every other week at the worship services, but never this close as she deliberately never walked in this couple's direction. Always away from them.

"What?" Levi said, slight impatience in his voice.

"Bart," she responded, her voice shaking some, "and his wife."

"Who?"

"Bart Altorfer," she hissed in a low voice, her face feeling warm. "I know you moved away several years ago to get married, but you must remember that he and I…. That we were together since before we finished school."

"*Yah*. I remember. Of course. Why didn't you marry? I know we don't talk about others' business, but the two of you seemed like a couple."

They stood in the middle of the *Englischer* fair, huddled together, talking in low tones. It was ridiculous.

"We were." She paused, giving the choking feeling in her throat a moment to subside and hoping furiously that she wasn't as red with embarrassment as she felt. "We were together, until Bart decided to marry Tabitha Brandenberger. She inherited her uncle's farm."

Straightening to look at her more fully, Levi's face reflected a shade of sympathy.

Not sure she cared for this, Dinah glared at him.

"Is this why you hang back? Because this *Mann* and his *Frau* are at the booth?"

Looking over Levi's shoulder, she met Bart's gaze and looked quickly away.

"Maybe. I've gone out of my way to avoid even speaking to them," she answered in a low, irritated voice.

Levi glanced at the food booth. "Our friends are working there and we know the food will be *gut*. Come on."

He took her hand again and began walking directly toward where Bart and Tabitha stood at the booth.

Trying to ignore the crazy zigzag of heat that ran up her arm, she let Levi Becker take her right up to the couple. Dragging him to a halt, she hissed to him, "Stop!"

"What?" he said in simple confusion, as if he had no awareness of her conflict.

"I'm not going over there," she said in a lowered tone. "What are you thinking?"

Levi gave her a serious look. "I think you shouldn't run from Bart anymore. If he took another woman for his *Frau,* more pity on him. Come on."

This time when he urged her forward, she let herself be pulled, her thoughts still scrambling. On one level, he was right.

Beside the food booth, there were several picnic tables set out for customers to settle in with their food. Out of the corner of her eye, Dinah noted that Bart and Tabitha had moved there to eat.

Breathing a little easier, since the *Mann* she'd thought to marry was no longer right ahead of her, Dinah took a deep breath, only dimly hearing Levi order food. When he then moved aside for those in line after her to step forward, she also shifted to the side.

She no longer had any feelings for Bart, but she'd never been treated as badly as when he dumped her and she didn't want anything to do with him. His rejection still stung a little, even though she thankfully no longer cared for him.

Gott did work wonders.

While Dinah was still lost in her thoughts, a *Frau* who she didn't recognize from their *Gmay* brought a sack of food to Levi.

Trailing after him, Dinah took several steps toward the picnic tables before she realized that Levi was settling at a table within feet of Brad and Tabitha.

"Come on." Levi gestured for her to come sit with him.

She swallowed and then, not knowing what else to do, sat down on the same side of the picnic tables. Levi sat next to her at the one table, between her and Bart, who sat with Tabitha at the next table.

For a while they two ate in silence, her boss glancing around like he hadn't a care in the world. Then Levi crumpled up his sandwich wrapper and thrust it in the bag. "Come on. Let's play corn hole."

"What?!" Dinah realized she was starting to sound like she only knew the one word.

Levi smiled at her. "Come play a game with me."

She stood by their table, unable to move and wanting to run.

Off in a fenced section behind the tables, two sets of corn hole boards were set up. An *Englischer* man and woman played together at the far set. The set of boards closest to Dinah and Levi were empty.

Dinah wavered. Just the day before a young *Buwe* had taught Levi to play the game.

She faced an almost certain embarrassment.

"Come." Despite his expression, his tone of voice was compelling.

The last thing she wanted was to appear silly in front of Bart and his *Frau*—to whom, she was sure, her former fiancé would have confessed their entire history. In many ways, she'd come to see Bart was a weak *Mann.*

"Come on." Levi's expression and his tone were now encouraging.

The *Englischer* couple finished their game, laughing as they walked out of the area, arm in arm.

Astonished, Dinah again let herself be pulled forward, but she couldn't tell this *Mann* that he faced embarrassment himself. As much as she had reason to dislike Levi, he was still her boss and she was still trying to be kind person, as *Gott* would want.

"Why? What are you doing?"

He'd just learned corn hole that morning—which was startling in itself as most all *Amische* knew the game—and now he wanted to have them play right in front of Bart and Tabitha!

Keeping her voice low, Dinah hissed, "No! I'm not playing!"

"*Yah.* We are." Levi bent to pick up the bean bags. "By the way, is Bart good at this game?"

"He's okay." She tried not to breathe too fast, although it was difficult.

"Are you good at corn hole?"

She glared at him. "I pitch for our soft ball games. *Yah*, I'm good at corn hole."

He gave her a broad smile. "Good. Come on, let's play."

"In front of Bart!" She tried not to screech, but it was hard.

Levi reached for her hand again, but this time she avoided his reach.

"I don't want to look like a fool in front of him." Dinah hissed, realizing that she was breathing faster now. She had to resist the urge to run right out of the corn hole enclosure.

"Come on, *Leibling*," Levi said loudly, "we don't want our onlookers to think we're fighting."

His use of this endearment made her pause, staring at him.

"Come on." Levi smiled, flashing a quick glance toward Bart, as if to let her in on something. "Let's play corn hole. I promise you won't regret it."

This last phrase was said in an even lower tone that she knew the couple watching them couldn't hear.

Feeling stuck between a rock and a hard place, Dinah took a step onto the corn hole grounds. Although, it occurred to her that she could just turn and walk away from this whole situation, the compelling look in Levi's eyes and the knowledge that Bart and Tabitha were most likely looking kept her there.

"Here," Levi said as she came stand near him. "Take the red bags and I'll take the blue."

His voice dipped lower again. "Do not worry if I appear, at first, to not know how to play."

"What?!" She knew he'd let a *Youngie* teach him the game only a day before!

"Shhhh," he responded.

"What!?" she repeated in a lowered voice.

"I said, do not worry if I appear not to know how to play the game. We want Bart to feel sure he can win, so he'll ask to play me."

"Oh! Okay." She still didn't know what Levi was up to, but he clearly had something planned.

"So, you're using those bean bags and I'll use these?" He said loudly, before hissing to her. "Take the other end."

Dinah had been playing cornhole since her older brother, Adam, taught her as a *Youngie*. This thing with Levi was another thing, though. She had no idea what he was up to, but she was curious to find out. For one thing, he seemed more open and…naive…than she'd ever known him to be.

"Okay. You stay here and toss the bags at the board at the other end. I'll go down there."

Feeling she'd played her part fairly well, she was glad to see the encouraging smile Levi gave her. She'd observed him smile like that with the kids that swarmed around him at the kick scooter shop. It lit up his whole face.

This looked like the Levi she'd known before.

"Alright," Levi said in that same simple voice, "is this how I toss them?"

Out of the corner of her eye, Dinah registered that Bart had come closer to watch them, his arms resting on the fence.

She firmed her jaw, suddenly flooded with the urge to bet him. *Gott* would certainly not be pleased as He'd directed them to be kind to their brethren. It streaked through her thoughts then that Bart didn't really deserve any consideration from her.

Taking a step forward as she tossed the bean bag underhand, Dinah let it go and watched the landing. Hitting right above one of the holes, the bean bag slid gently down through the hole.

"Ooch! That was a good one!" Levi called out. "Okay, my turn."

When the bag that he threw hit the side of the cornhole board and fell off, she stood there watching and wondering if she were an idiot to do this with him. In front of Bart, who she knew from their time together played a competent corn hole game.

Receiving another cheery smile from Levi, she made no response when he called. "I'm getting better at this game."

Dinah sent him a weak smile, very conscious of Bart leaning against the fence as he watched them play.

"Your turn," Levi called, seeming unconcerned that they had an audience.

The rest of the game went just as badly with Dinah beating Levi every inning. She threw and usually got her bag in the top hole, but at least it never fell off the board. He, however, trailed after her, not seeming worried that he had an audience.

Halfway through the game, they switched positions and Dinah rigidly made sure she didn't look at Bart when she passed him.

The match ended after an ugly second half. She could have cried, but controlled her face, not wanting to give Bart any satisfaction. Confronted with the two of them together, she decided that he was a bigger jerk than Levi.

Just as they were—to Dinah's relief—leaving the corn hole set up, a voice called out.

"Say, friend!"

Swiveling toward Bart, anger and dread flooded her.

He was looking at Levi, an oily smile on his face.

She wondered how she could have ever considered spending her life with this *Mann*. Had he always been like this?

"*Hallo*," Levi responded.

She squinted at him a little, trying to make sense of his friendly *Deerich* expression as he looked at Bart.

"How about a game?" Bart responded. "Just you and I. Your lady can sit here with my *Frau*."

Not if there was nowhere else to stand!

She moved to a spot on the other side of the enclosure.

Watching the two men, Dinah was suddenly flooded with shame that she'd ever considered marrying Bart. The *Bisskatz* was specifically singling out a beginner at the game! He had to have seen Levi's level of play, had to know he could beat him.

"Okay!" Levi responded, turning to her to say after a moment, "I won't keep you long."

Knowing there was little hope of it, she spitefully wished Levi would beat Bart handily. Bart deserved it.

With lagging feet, she turned and went to sit at the further picnic table where they'd eaten, leaving Tabitha at the far end. She couldn't keep from watching the two *Menner* in the cornhole enclosure, though.

"You take this end…."

She heard only dimly the directions Bart gave Levi. Like he was directing a lamb to the fleecing. It made her sick inside.

Bart's *Frau*, however, showed only an encouraging smile.

That made Dinah nauseated, too.

No wonder Bart had grown into such a *Schlang*, with a wife like Tabitha. She clearly didn't bring out the best in him.

In the corn hole court, Levi swung one of his bags back and forth, like a total beginner who was warming up.

Dinah was dimly aware of the noise beyond the food both and was even startled by her *Gershwinder*, surprised when Adam and Naomi appeared at her elbow. "*Hallo*! What are you two doing here?"

She asked the question absently, though, hardly able to turn her eyes away from the horrible match in front of her.

In glancing at her siblings, she saw Adam gently pull one of Naomi's bonnet strings. "I'd picked her up from visiting with the twins at the Schwartentruber *Haus* when she saw the fair as we drove home. She just had to come see the fair."

Looking back over her shoulder at the corn hole game, Dinah quickly swung her gaze back to her little sister and Adam. "It's just a silly *Englischer* fair, you know."

"Then why are you here?" Naomi asked in a perky voice.

Just then Dinah heard Bart cry out in success and she turned to see him shouting for himself. To her side, Tabitha cheered him, sounding like she'd won the game herself.

Giving a disgusted grunt, Dinah glanced over at the man with whom she'd come to this *Englischer* fair. Adam and Naomi were forgotten in that moment.

Oddly, Levi just smiled with satisfaction and then suggested—in that same silly voice that didn't sound like him—that they play again.

It came as no surprise to Dinah that Bart quickly agreed.

"Are you staying to watch?" Her brother asked in a quiet tone.

Dinah wasn't sure what to do. While part of her wanted nothing more than to walk away from this travesty, she hesitated to leave Levi to face this alone.

While she stood there, wavering, he called out to her. "Dinah! Are you leaving?"

She looked at him, standing now at the other end of the corn hole court.

"Stay," Levi called out to her, something in his expression compelling.

For a long moment, she locked eyes with him, the hurt she'd endured after Bart's rejection pushing hard on her heart.

"Stay," Levi said again.

"Dinah?" her brother said after a moment.

Patting his arm in a gesture to reassure him, Dinah hoisted herself onto the picnic table in a way that would have probably drawn a rebuke from her mother for being unladylike.

"I'm here," she said, "go ahead with the game."

"Glad you didn't leave?" Levi asked her as he drove his buggy away from the fairgrounds an hour later.

In the waning light, he saw her turn to face him.

"You've played corn hole before."

Her conclusion stated the obvious as he'd won handily in his second and third games against the *Mann* with whom she'd once courted. Levi drew in a deep breath, knowing with a smile on his face that *Gott* would forgive him this once. If anyone knew how Bart had hurt Dinah, it was *Gott*. Levi didn't know the whole of it, but the look on her face when she'd seen Bart had told him all he needed to know.

Suddenly, he'd wanted to trounce the *Mann*.

"Many times," Levi agreed with her statement.

"Not just yesterday when you let young Micah 'teach' you."

"*Neh.*"

"Why then did you act with the *Buwe* like you'd never learned to play?"

Staring over his horse's ears as he directed the buggy, Levi glanced over at her.

"Micah needed to feel big and strong. He needed to teach me, so I let him."

They trotted into the shadow of tall trees overhead and she said nothing for a while.

"You planned this with Bart."

Her tone was hard to read. "*Yah*. Does that upset you?"

Maybe she still had feelings for the *Mann*? Considering the possibility uneasily, Levi looked at it now. He'd actually never thought about that.

"No," she responded. "Some would say you weren't honest in what you did…."

Taking a deep breath—because it sounded like she still had feelings for Bart—Levi glanced away from the road to slash her a look. In the dim spring light inside the buggy, she appeared to be smiling.

"I'm not one of them," Dinah said, "I think Bart only played with you because he thought he could beat you. That makes him the worse."

"Yes." It was silly to be so relieved that she wasn't still enamored of the jerk.

"Why?" She furrowed her brow as she looked over at him.

Levi looked away from her to the lane ahead. "I don't think bullies should get away with doing bad things."

"Oh."

"And you seem like a nice young woman," the sentence trailed out of him in a mumbled voice.

A peal of laughter erupted from the girl next to him.

"Well, don't say it like you're so much older! *Denki*, by the way. I appreciate what you did."

He looked at her again. "Like I said. He deserved it."

"It's not like any real harm was done to him," Dinah said. "Just to his feelings and he never would have gotten beaten so badly, if he hadn't put himself into the situation with you."

They trotted on in silence.

"Look," she said suddenly. "Thank you."

Levi felt a smile curve his mouth. "You're welcome. Any time."

That evening, Dinah spooned in a bite of Abby's soup, made with early summer squash. "I have no idea why Levi did what he did with Bart. Honestly, I was just glad to see Bart brought down a peg or two."

"I guess he's not all bad then. *Gott* gives us all different gifts," Abigail commented from where she washed the pot in the kitchen sink.

"Maybe," Dinah responded, "but Levi seems so cold and unfriendly to most. He certainly wasn't that way today."

"Not to you, for sure" Adam said, sitting across the table.

"Or the children who come to the shop," Abby pointed out. "At least, it didn't sound that way from what you said the other day."

"Maybe I was wrong about him," mused Dinah, perplexed by the different sides of the *Mann*. Lately, she'd been feeling almost concerned for him. He wasn't perfect, but he didn't deserve to live a life without love, either. By having decided to enter into another marriage only without love, he'd be cheating himself.

Abby was silent and Dinah looked at her with concern. Her sister didn't show her feelings often, but that didn't mean they weren't there. Sometimes her sister seemed almost too perfect.

"Not likely," her *Bruder* said. "Maybe he's being nice to his customers and, you said, he needs your help in the shop."

"I know and he said that mean thing about Gabe."

Abigail glanced over at the two at the table. “Remember, he said nothing that wasn’t true. *Gott* forgives us all our moments of transgression.”

Dinah got up from the table, taking her bowl to the sink. She knew the answer, but asked anyway. “Have you forgiven him?”

An ironic smile curled Abby’s mouth. “*Yah*, of course.”

“Sister,” Adam stood up to bring his bowl for washing, “have you forgiven yourself? Are your requirements of yourself more than *Gott* requires. We’re taught that He loves us, even though we are not worthy.”

Dinah looked at them without saying anything, hoping Abby could hear the reason in Adam’s words.

“I’m trying, but I’m not there yet,” Abigail admitted, giving their brother a crooked smile. “Maybe urging Dinah to forgive Levi is part of forgiving myself.”

A week later, Dinah stood at the end of the counter, drying cups she and Levi used for water. There were several *Youngies* in the shop looking at the kick scooters on a display table.

At the other end of the counter, Levi and Micah Spanky looked over a small stack of books the *Buwe* had brought with him.

Dinah tried not to stare at them, wondering what their hushed conversation was about. Every now and then, Micah looked over at the other boys.

“That’s great, Micah.” Levi stacked the colorful books, turning to place them on a shelf behind the counter. “Tell me which you liked the best.”

The boy seemed to ponder. “I think the one about the caterpillar that ate everything.”

“That is a good one.” Again, he seemed warm with his young customers. Dinah couldn’t help staring.

She’d seen him like this many times in recent weeks, but this Levi was so different than the one at Sings or church.

"Do I get the kick scooter now?"

Even though, he spoke in a low tone, Micah's clear voice carried and Dinah looked up from her task, wondering if she'd heard right.

"*Yah*, of course you do. That was the deal, right. I said that you get the scooter when the books were read."

"It was hard," confessed the boy, "but the books were funny. Particularly that caterpillar one. I liked the one about the rabbit, too."

Levi smiled. "I'm glad."

"The teacher could hardly believe it," Micah said, clearly liking that he'd achieved this.

Reaching over to a kick scooter that was propped on the counter as a display, Levi grabbed it and handed the scooter to Micah. "Here you are."

His eyes glistening, the boy hugged the thing to his chest.

"Now, you must practice riding it, so you can go easily."

"I will! I promise I will!"

"Come on out," called Simon Hahn. "I'll teach you!"

With that, Micah ran out of the shop, several of the other *Kinder* following.

Mark Hahn's story was looking more and more false.

Compelled, Dinah moved down the counter to say, "You made a deal with Micah Spanky that you'd give him a kick scooter?"

Levi looked over, his expression now flat. "*Yah*."

A shout from the group of other *Buwe* near a table by the front window drew Dinah's attention before she turned back to Levi, determined to get the full picture. "You promised him a scooter if he read some books? Why?"

"Because his *familye* doesn't have much money. He's the youngest of fourteen and I offered him a way to get himself a kick scooter."

"Yet, this is how you make your money. Selling these to the other *Buwe*."

Nodding, Levi agreed. "Micah, also, has difficulty learning to read. He told me this once when no one else was in the shop. That was back when my sister worked here. It's taken him some time to get through all the books."

"Are you sure he did?" Dinah looked sideways at him.

Levi's brows lifted. "He gave me the books back, claiming to have read each one. He didn't know if I'd quiz him to find if he was truthful."

"But, you didn't."

"*Neh*, I trusted him."

"Why? He could have just wanted the scooter."

"*Yah*. I'm leaving the matter to *Gott*...and to Micah. It is my choice to trust him."

For several long minutes, Dinah examined his face. This side of Levi was very different than she'd expected of him. Not the new Levi. It had to be a deviation though.

The *Mann* who was cold and unfriendly, who had said the harsh words that hurt Abby, must be nicer to *Kinder*, that was all.

He had set up the cornhole situation with Bart, though. It all left her very confused.

A week later, Levi found himself watching Dinah. Without much thought on how he'd format the question, he blurted out, "Exactly how many *Menner* are you seeing?"

She looked up from tallying last month's sales. "What?"

Straightening his coat lapels, he said, "Well, I saw you drive home last Sunday from the *Gmay* with Hiram Reese. It just made me wonder, that's all."

"None of your business!" she retorted after a moment.

He shrugged, lifted his brows. "I'd think that since you rejected my proposal—"

She snorted.

"—and I lowered Bart's conceit at cornhole, that I'd have the right to ask that question, at least," he said mildly, tinkering with a kick scooter on the counter.

Out of the corner of his eye, he saw Dinah give him a considering glance.

"Well, doesn't it?" he questioned.

"Maybe," she responded ungraciously, "but that doesn't mean I want to answer."

Levi frowned. "There are only so many *Menner* in the area. Don't you know how many you're seeing?"

"Of course, I do!" This was said with indignation.

He shook his head, hiding a smile. "You're driving out with all the ones in this area, aren't you. I can see why you wouldn't want to say that."

"I'm not!"

"Then why won't you give me a number?"

"Because," she snapped, a little more loudly, "it's none of your business!"

He didn't know why he was teasing her about this. Levi supposed he liked seeing Dinah all spirited in her reaction.

"That's fine," he said, "I can understand."

"I don't think you do," she responded. "Just why do you want to know, anyway?"

Levi recognized that he should have seen this question coming, but he hadn't. "Oh, I suppose I wanted to offer—to offer some assistance."

"What?" She looked astonished. "How? Are you sure you aren't still convincing me that—at my age—I ought to settle into a loveless marriage with you?"

He waved a dismissive hand. "*Neh*, I think you were right to refuse to consider the idea."

The more he thought of it, Levi thought he might have liked being married to this *Maedel*. That would never do. He needed someone very different, although he couldn't say how.

Dinah looked at him, her face still suspicious. "You do?"

"Yes." He was making this up as he went along, because he surely couldn't tell her that he liked her too much to marry. "I've just come to feel we are becoming friends and I want to help you find the right husband."

She looked at him, as if considering whether he was truthful in what he said. “You want to…to help? How?”

“*Menner* talk.” He looked over at her with another shrug. “We probably shouldn’t, but we do and men know things about other men.”

“Things?”

“*Yah*, like who talks more kindly about *Mamms* and sisters. That sort of thing. The kind of thing that *Maedels* listen for.”

“You want to help me know which might be the best husband?”

“I do,” he said, as the words came out of his mouth, Levi wondered what he was letting himself in for?

CHAPTER FIVE

Two days later, she stood on the porch at the back of Levi's shop, banging dust out of a rug that hung over the rail there.

She knew he'd done enough to make her dislike him, but Dinah was confused. She'd also seen him do some nice things. He'd sometimes seemed like the Levi of earlier times.

Awkwardly grabbing the rug, she turned and headed back inside.

Levi sat on the tall stool next to his work bench, sanding one of the small wooden toys he made.

Turning toward her when she marched into the shop's back room, Levi said, after a hesitant moment. "You told me that you and Bart broke up when he decided to marry this other woman. I can see how that must have hurt, but that may not have stopped you from caring for him. You liked him before, do you now still have feelings for him? Is that why you haven't chosen another *Mann* to court with?"

"No," she responded with a snap. "And this is none of your business!"

He shook his head, apparently unmoved by her rebuke. "You have driven out with several. Menner obviously like you."

"I don't see that this is any of your business!" Her vigorous words trailing off, she turned to straighten the now dustless rug on the floor.

"Really? Even after I beat Bart so thoroughly at corn hole? Come on!" This was said in a surprisingly teasing tone.

"Why do you ask? It can have nothing to do with you." Dinah swallowed, feeling embarrassed to tell him her dilemma.

Levi waited a moment before saying, "Can no other *Mann* measure up to him? Surely, this is not the case."

She ducked her head, her mouth tight shut. It was hateful to remember what a fool she'd been. The thought of making such a mistake again made her shudder.

"Since you've worked here," he paused, "you've driven out with several *Menner*. You must have found some you like."

"*Yah*." Honestly, she didn't know why she was telling him anything. It just seemed like he had earned the right to know...he seemed interested. "I was wrong about Bart."

She swallowed before saying, "Maybe I did something wrong. Something to make him marry Tabitha. I don't know and I just can't judge who is safest to trust."

Levi slewed around on his stool. "Really? You? No. This was Bart's choice. You said it—he married a woman with a farm, Tabitha Brandenberger."

"Okay," she shot back. "That then says something about his character that I didn't see. I could be wrong again! Besides, you did nothing to cause Anna's death, but you're determined not to face that again."

"I am." He frowned, saying after a moment, "You were young when you started courting with Bart."

"Maybe. No younger than other girls.

"I don't remember a Brandenberger family hereabouts," he mused.

Making a face, Dinah said, "Probably not. Tabitha's *Onkel* was John Gindelsberger. She inherited the farm from him."

"Oh. John Gindelsberger, the single *Mann* who frowned at everyone? I wonder if Tabitha is like her *Onkel*. He left his farm to her? That won't hurt a girl in finding a husband. If a *Mann* were to choose his *Frau* that way."

After another pause, Levi added, "I wouldn't have thought it of Bart, either."

She added nothing, not knowing what to say. She'd gotten over Bart soon after his real character had been made clear, but the subject still stung, a little, and it left her with this big predicament.

Levi gave a rusty laugh, saying, "I know many *Amische* families have names with a similar sound, but you have to admit that Brandenberger and Gindelsberger are very alike. Both Bergers."

His comment was so unexpected that Dinah found herself chuckling in response.

Later that morning, as she worked alongside Levi, Dinah found herself praying silently, "*Dear Gott, help me know how to see this. I witnessed Abby crying after Levi's remark. I've seen him be cold and unfriendly to others. I have even heard bad things about Levi.*

She lifted her gaze to rest on the *Mann* across the room and then went on with her prayer. *I have also seen him be kind to children, despite Mark Hahn's claim. He's even been kind to me—in what he did with Bart. Help me, Lord, help me know how to…"*

Dinah let her prayerful thoughts trail off, knowing that *Gott* saw more than she could ever see, knew more what she meant than she knew, at this moment.

A week and a half later, Abby asked her, "How was your drive out with Jethro Wedel?"

"Okay." Dinah sat at the kitchen table folding clothes she'd just pulled off the clothesline. Abby stood at the stove, stirring the stew for supper.

"Only okay?"

At that moment, Faith ran through the kitchen, banging the back door behind her as she galloped out.

Mamm followed their youngest sister into the room, calling out the door, "Don't forget to sweep the porch before you let the chickens out for their pen time."

"You should probably remind her to check their nests for eggs again," Abby commented.

Their *Mamm* came back to sit at the kitchen table with Dinah. "I probably should have, but, no doubt, she's halfway down the road to visit Eve."

Turning to glance over her shoulder, Abby made a face, "It's good she has a friend who lives so close, but it seems like she's always over at the Imhoff *Haus*."

Dinah said nothing, glad that her elder sister's questions were no longer directed at her.

"I think it is a *gut* thing that Faith's friend lives right next door," their *Mamm* responded. "We always know where she is and that she'll be well fed."

Abby snorted. "That's one good thing about her being at Eve's. We don't have to feed her."

Not able to keep from commenting, Dinah added, "Except when Faith and Eve are here and then we feed both."

"Have you told *Mamm* about your 'okay' drive with Jethro?"

Cursing herself for opening her mouth about the subject, Dinah hunched over the clothes' basket. She hadn't even talked with her *familye* about her problem and she had no idea why she'd told Levi.

"Now, Abby, this isn't our business to discuss. Dinah will tell us if she's to join with a *Mann*." *Mamm's* tone was kind and warm.

"*Mamm*!" Dinah burst into speech. "Do you think something is wrong with me because I can't decide on a *Buwe* to court with?"

"Of course, not!" her mother said, pressing Dinah's hand.

"Abby married early—"

"And you see where that got me," her sister inserted.

"Only because your husband died! You couldn't help that," Dinah said in response.

"Well, you couldn't help Bart choosing to marry that woman with the farm," Abby tossed back, using one hand to stir the soup.

"It's understandable that you both want to take your time finding another *Mann*," *Mamm* concluded. "Was the drive with Jethro bad?"

"*Neh*. Just boring," Dinah responded with frustration.

"That's too bad. You've known him since the two of you were *Bopplin*. Maybe you were too close." Her mother got up to peer into the stew pot.

"Maybe." Still wrestling with the question she'd asked her mother, Dinah fell silent.

"You agreed to drive out with him, though," Abby pointed out after their mother had tasted the stew before sprinkling in more salt. "You must have some interest in him."

The clothes all folded, Dinah sat with her hands in her lap. "I was—I don't know—hoping to see him differently."

All three women were silent for several moments before Abby said, "Some women marry to have a home and children. That's all."

Dinah looked at her. "I know. I tell myself that."

"Don't," their mother said in a tart voice. "You're both too smart to have that kind of marriage. It usually leaves a bad taste in your mouth. Besides, women usually do this when they have no home, no other choice. You neither one have this problem."

Abby set the stew spoon on a spoon rest. "What if you want a home of your own? Kinder? That's a reason to marry for practical reasons."

Saying nothing, Dinah reflected that her *Mamm* was right. She and Abby both were blessed to have *Gott* provide this loving home.

Her mother moved to leave the kitchen. "You both have nothing to worry about. You each will find just the right *Menner* for you. I believe that *Gott* has that planned for you."

"It's all right," Dinah said to her *Schweschder* after their mother had gone into the living room "I may not find a *Mann*. I'll stay here to care for *Mamm* and *Daed*."

Abby erupted into laughter. "I think it's too early for you to plan that. Just because the drive with Jethro didn't go well."

Dinah looked down at her folded hands. "None of them seem to go well."

"Still," her sister came over to pat her shoulder, "we just need to have faith and keep living our lives. I'm sure one of the *Menner* who ask to drive out with you will be the right one."

After the luncheon served after the next meeting of his *Gmay*, Levi leaned against a shade tree at the Kauffman *Haus*, talking to his friend, Aaron. As it had grown warm with the approaching summer, his discarded hat lay on the ground a foot away.

"I'm glad your business is doing well," Aaron said, a toothpick dangling from the corner of his mouth. "Kids deserve kick scooters."

Levi grinned at him. "Do you even know where yours is or do you still use it?"

As his friend chuckled, Aaron responded, "I'm the youngest of eight *Kinder*. By the time the last kick scooter got to me, it was in sad shape. The wheel bearings were shot and the handle finally fell off totally."

As the two men were under a tree in an empty pasture next to the Kauffman *Haus*, families and couples kept trailing past, headed to the buggies parked in that space.

"Oh, sad *Buwe*," Levi teased. "You probably didn't have any toys."

"Not true." Aaron spit out the toothpick. "Although my brothers and sisters had already worn out a scooter before the one I was given, there were other toys. I fondly remember a top that Daniel, the eldest of our family, you know, whittled for me. It was the best."

Another family walked past the two, clearly headed toward their buggy to head home after the luncheon.

Levi noticed that a small girl slept on the father's shoulder. A pang went through him at the sight, but he'd learned to ignore this feeling. "That was kind of Daniel."

"*Yah*," Aaron shifted to lean more comfortably against the tree trunk. "I'm told I was a very sweet, calm *Bopplin*."

Laughter bursting out of him at this matter-of-fact statement, Levi slapped his knee.

"Isn't that Dinah Zook headed out in that buggy with Moses Drissell?" Aaron asked.

Startled by the question, Levi looked in the direction his friend pointed, seeing that it was, in fact, Dinah seated next to Moses as a buggy headed out of the parking area.

She was still trying to find a *Mann* she could trust, he registered.

"Levi?" Aaron asked after a moment. "Did you hear what I said?"

"*Yah*," Levi responded finally, telling himself that it was no business of his who Dinah drove out with. She'd already rejected his proposal and it wasn't as if he loved her. "I suppose she's working out well."

"You suppose?" His friend asked, a hint of laughter in his voice. "You don't know?"

Shrugging, he said, "Dinah's doing fine."

She was doing better than that, he admitted to himself. She'd made some good changes to the place.

"And the two of you are getting along okay? I mean, you said, when Esther married, that you needed no one to work in the shop with you."

"Well, I'm sure I could do things all myself—"

"But you like having Dinah working there with you?"

Levi paused before saying. "Yes, I do. She seems like a good girl."

"I'm glad to know it's working out," Aaron commented, his broad hat dangling from his hand.

Having mulled over things for a moment, Levi said, "She's actually become a friend, of sorts."

"Of sorts?" The laughter was again evident in Aaron's question.

With another shrug, Levi said, "Dinah is still working for me, that makes this a little different than you and I."

"That and the fact that she's a *Maedel.*"

"Yes," responded Levi in a dry voice. "That is different."

The next day, Dinah sat fuming behind the counter, irritated that Levi Becker was again being a jerk. Why did he seem this way with some, but not with the children who came here?

Across the shop, Levi stood beside Hiram Reese, her friend Mary's brother, stiff and unsmiling as Hiram asked about a kick scooter. Apparently, the younger Reese boy was having a birthday and the *familye* was looking to buy him a gift.

Levi's unfriendliness with Hiram made Mark Hahn's story seem likely! Although, she now doubted it totally. She'd seen his son with Levi.

"And this scooter is strong?" Hiram asked, seeming unaware that Levi wasn't being very friendly.

"*Yah.* It's one of the best we have."

Hadn't they all grown up together? He knew Hiram, probably not all that well and certainly not recently. There might have been some excuse for his behavior, if the two were strangers, though, they were taught to welcome all.

Twenty minutes later, when Hiram had completed his purchase and left the shop, Dinah went to stand in front of the stool where Levi had perched, her hand on her hip.

"What?" He glanced up from the counter, looking as if he were completely unaware of how he'd acted with Mary's *Bruder*.

"What?" She echoed with sarcasm. "You were so cold and unfriendly, just now! It's a wonder that you have any customers. You're that way with all the grown-ups who come here. It's just the *Kinder* that get the friendly you. Honestly, you have two different sides!"

Staring at her blankly, Levi responded, "I have no idea what you mean."

"Of course, you don't! Do you even know how unkind and unfriendly you can be?"

"Unkind?"

Near to sputtering, Dinah swallowed and took a deep breath. "*Yah*. Unkind. Well, cold and not friendly."

"How is this so?"

"You said that mean thing about Gabe Eichelberger having died with no children! And you said this right where my sister—Gabe's widow—heard you!"

Levi's cheeks grew a little flushed, but he retorted, "We've talked about this. I didn't know your sister could hear, and Gabe did die childless. That's a fact."

"It is, but you didn't have to stress that in front of Abby!" Dinah stormed. "She cried, after she heard what you said, cried! Abby never cries."

"Her husband had died," Levi snapped. "It's natural that she should cry."

"My sister doesn't show others what she's feeling! I found her crying in private behind the Nussbaum *Haus*."

He was silent for a moment, his face without expression.

"This is why I could never think of marrying you!" she stormed. "I had a hard time coming to work here, not wanting to seem disloyal to Abby!"

Levi still said nothing, his jaw tight, as if he were clenching it. "I'm sorry. I didn't intend to cause anyone pain."

A loaded silence fell between them before he added, "I know what it is to love and lose. I understand your sister's distress."

She hardly registered what he said. "Just like you don't intend to be unfriendly to the grown-ups that come in here!"

"What? Unfriendly to our customers?" He glared at her. "Because I don't ask them into the back room and offer them coffee?"

His derision rolled over Dinah and she repeated, "This is why I refused to marry you! I mean, I probably would have refused anyway, but I had many reasons to do so."

"And this is what you think of me," he said after a moment. "I'm sorry if I offended your sister. I didn't know she was close enough to hear my comment. I never meant to give her pain. Please handle the shop. There is need of me elsewhere."

CHAPTER SIX

Walking home quickly after work that evening, Dinah sprinted up the stairs. She found her youngest sister, Faith, tending to the supper preparations in the kitchen under their *Grossmammie's* eye. When she saw Abby wasn't there, Dinah went into the living room, calling for her.

Levi's apology hadn't been enthusiastic or lengthy, and Dinah didn't know if he'd been sincere, but she wanted to tell her sister about it, anyway.

"Abby? Abby?"

"Here, up in *Mamm* and *Daed's* room," Abigail answered.

Dinah breathlessly bounded in, coming to a halt next to her parents' bed.

Her *Schweschder* stood on the other side of the mattress, flapping a white top sheet over the mattress. "What has you in such a rush?"

"I'm just home from work." She paused to catch her breath.

Her sister's smile was characteristically ironical. "*Yah.* We are all glad, I'm sure."

Flopping down on the unmade bed—wrinkling the top sheet as she did so—Dinah announced, "Levi apologized!"

Shooing her off the bed, Abby went on tucking in the sheet. "He did? For what?"

Dinah quirked her mouth to the side before responding. "What he said that day that got you so upset. That Gabe had died without children. As if you'd deliberately kept him from becoming a *Daed*!"

Retrieving the quilt to smooth out over the bed, her sister stopped, regarding her with a flat expression. "He didn't 'get me upset'. It is a reality that Gabe and I didn't have *Kinder*."

"Yes, but Levi didn't have to say it that way when you could overhear him. Anyway, that's not the point. He apologized!"

"Why would he do that?"

Abby's question was said in a disinterested voice, but Dinah knew that this event had made her stoic sister cry. "Because I told him how mean that was."

"You did?"

"He's so unfriendly, so cold to grown-ups and you aren't the only person he's been ugly with. Remember that I told you what Mark Hahn said about Levi and Mark's son? Not that I believe this after seeing him with children, but still."

"I do remember." Abby fluffed the pillows before placing them again in *Mamm* and *Daed's* bed. "I don't know Mark Hahn very well, but it's not a good thing when information is passed about another."

Dinah frowned. "I know. He seemed very believable to me, though I know now that he didn't tell the truth."

"You also said that Levi is kind to the children that come to the shop? Why, you told me that he even let the one boy teach him to play corn hole, although he knew how all along? Why would he do so with one child, but cheat another one?"

"I know," Dinah said slowly. "I don't know what to make of him, really. He was so stiff and unfriendly with Hiram just this morning."

Her sister gave her a look to indicate she didn't follow.

"Hiram Reese—Mary's brother. He came in to buy a kick scooter for the younger *Kinder* in the *familye*. One of the children has a birthday soon."

"Oh. Yes."

Dinah shook her head. "Levi was so different with him. I don't know."

Clutching to her chest another quilt that her parents could use when the nights grew cooler, she stared into air. "I just can't make him out. He's so nice sometimes—"

"—like when he beat Bart at corn hole after finding out what a jerk Bart was to you—"

—and sometimes he's not friendly, at all."

"I guess this is why we are not to judge others," Abby observed rationally. "*Gott* sees the heart, but we cannot."

"I know," Dinah responded, her tone tart, "but this makes it hard to know what to believe and who to trust. Remember, I trusted Bart and he turned on me."

"Would you trust him again?"

"No," she responded in exasperation, "I wouldn't, but I don't know how to judge Levi's sincerity…or any other *Mann's*."

"And yet, you think he may truly feel badly about what he said?" Abigail looked down.

Dinah couldn't believe she was saying this, "I do, I guess."

Her sister looked up. "That would make him less objectionable, wouldn't it?"

"Maybe." She drew the word out.

"I guess we'll just have to see."

"I suppose so, but I don't think we were wrong about him…and I don't think he'll bring this up again." Dinah moved to the bedroom door. "I know he's still unfriendly to most adults. It's hard to believe I could have measured his character so far from the truth."

The next Friday afternoon, Levi stared at Dinah as she sat across from him in the shop's back room. It had come to him several days ago, as he watched her drive away with another young *Mann* from their *Gmay*, that he might as well help her. Afterall, he'd had a happy marriage. Before the tragedy ended it all.

Please, Gott. I know you're there. Help me to understand.

He took a deep breath.

Dinah had refused to join him in a loveless marriage and her one false step with Bart seemed to be making it hard for her to move forward.

He had been struggling to find the right moment to talk with her about this and he'd said something that once. He'd not been sure he should say more that day and then *Youngies* seem to crowd the shop often. On two evenings, she'd left on her various buggy drives with different *Menner* taking her home.

One of those afternoons, she'd been driven home by young Abel Stover. The *Buwe* had been behind her one grade, if Levi remembered right. She had been behind him in school and he was sure that Abel had been behind her.

She never drove home with a *Mann* twice, from what he could see, and Levi wondered if she'd run out of *Menner* soon.

Now, they were alone, sitting together in the back room at their various tasks.

Levi cleared his throat in preparation—and then cleared it again to get her attention.

Engaged in stitching a dress for one of the faceless dolls she'd recently suggested they offer for sale in the shop, Dinah looked up.

"You drove home with young Abel Stover the other day?" he said, immediately regretting that he'd phrased this as a question.

"*Yah.*" She looked down again at her stitching.

"Is he the *Buwe* you've been looking for?" he asked, again cringing at his own question.

Dinah looked at him a moment before returning her gaze to the fabric in her hands.

"I don't know. Probably not. Why?" She returned with her own question, leaving him to swallow hard before he spoke again.

"You know that Anna and I were only married a short time."

"Yes, I knew you were only gone from here several years before you returned."

"Three." It was surprisingly comfortable to talk with her about this. He hadn't really spoken to anyone about his ill-fated marriage, if he could call it that. He'd never believed that *Gott* did evil in the world, although He certainly allowed it to happen.

Levi looked down. "I loved Anna."

He glanced up to see Dinah's compassionate gaze resting on him. Good, he thought. He didn't want her to see his addressing of her *Menner*-situation as criticism.

"I have loved," he said. "I can understand that you're looking for the right person."

"Someone not like Bart."

"*Neh*. Different. Has it not seemed that any of the *Menner* you've driven out with are to be trusted?"

She didn't respond for a few minutes and Levi sat listening to the silence between them, only stirred by the sound of the gentle breeze that came through the back door. Maybe he shouldn't have brought this up.

"How do I know?" For a moment, she looked at him, her blue eyes troubled. "I don't know."

Slowly, he responded, "There are signs. Did you see nothing in Bart—before his betrayal—that troubled you?"

Frowning at the doll dress in her hands, Dinah exhaled.

"In looking back, I can see now that he wasn't always honest, but I was…young. There was much I didn't notice."

Levi felt a smile curve his lips. "You still are young."

"Not that young…or naïve."

She lay her stitchery aside, getting up for a drink from the covered water jug that sat in the corner. "Bart and I started driving out when I was hardly more than a *Youngie*."

This was often the case in their world.

"*Yah*."

Dinah turned to look at him. "I got familiar with Bart. I didn't see him as more than.... just Bart. I had niggling concerns, but I ignored them."

"Until he married Tabitha?"

"Yes. Then I reflected. I saw it then, that he'd often taken shortcuts, told others little lies. It hadn't seemed so terrible at the time."

Feeling compelled, Levi asked, "Do you still love him? Even now?"

She barked a laugh, almost before the words were out of his mouth. "*Neh.* No, not at all. But don't you see? How do I know, now, what it is to love? I know what it is to not love! I look back and see that I never loved him, not the way a *Maedel* is to love a husband, you know? At least, that's what it seems. I don't know!"

"I see that, but how are you to ever make a choice between these *Menner*, if you only drive out with each the one time?"

"I don't know that, either!" she exclaimed, coming back to drop down on her stool in exasperation. "Shouldn't I feel some interest in them beyond friendship? Some flicker of something?"

He took a minute before responding. "It is difficult."

Clearing his throat, he said. "Remember, I do know what it is to love."

She looked at him.

Talking about this had felt awkward at first, but now that he'd started, Levi realized he felt better. "Tell me what you've learned since truly seeing Bart for what he is."

"Well," Dinah said slowly, "What I said, mostly."

"Is Bart anything like your *Daed*?"

Bristling at that, she immediately shot back, "What do you mean? My *Daed* is wonderful to my *Mamm*…and to us all! He's nothing like Bart. *Daed* would never tell even a small lie!"

They sat, facing one another across the shop, her looking at him indignantly.

"I didn't say that he wasn't wonderful. Did you ever compare Bart to you father?"

She lifted her brows. "No, I don't suppose I did."

"Okay," Levi said, "that's a start. You could do that when considering a *Mann*. Have you ever asked a friend what they think of these *Menner*?"

Dinah shook her head, grimacing at him. "That would seem awkward. I'm not asking my friends to pass judgement on these *Menner*. They know them all. Some are their *Bruders*!"

"Of course, not. We are told not to pass judgement," he responded, "but *Gott* has also directed us to marry and be fertile. *Gott* knows this means we will have to make choices between others."

"It still feels awkward."

"That may be, but you seem to be stuck. Not able to choose. Not sure which is best."

Looking at him with a glum expression, Dinah said, "*Yah*. I am exactly there."

He shrugged. "Okay, talk with me about these different *Menner*. My sisters are all married and I have no brothers for you to consider."

"What?" she yelped.

"Look, I have nothing in this. Your choice is your choice, but talking to me might help you see your own feelings."

"I have family," she retorted, "my parents, my brothers and sisters. Even my *Grossmammie*."

"Yes, you do and yet you keep driving out with a new *Mann* every time."

She dropped her head. "I guess I keep thinking I'll feel something with someone."

"You probably will, but it can't hurt to make use of me." He didn't know why he was so insistent about this. He'd seen her distress and stepped up already to beat Bart at corn hole, although beating Bart at the game had been as fun for him as it had been for her to watch.

She'd find someone on her own, but this way, he felt he was putting a buffer between them, too.

This way he was safely off the list of options. Everyone won.

She gave him a long look. "Okay, I will accept your help. *Denki*."

The next Saturday night, Dinah lay in her bed with the quilts tucked under her chin, listening to the wind wailing outside. Across the room, her sisters, Naomi and Faith slept, their breathing regular. She could tell, however, that Abby was awake, like her.

"It sounds like a gale whipping up outside," Dinah whispered, just as raindrops began hitting the window hard.

"Yes, it does."

Dinah fell silent, her thoughts returning to Levi's unexpected words on Friday afternoon. She'd thought about his offer all day while she worked around the *Haus*.

There were always many things to be done on the weekends, but the work hadn't stopped her thoughts. Not only had she been surprised to have Levi offer to sort through her *Menner* challenge, but he'd also seemed to understand what she had been afraid to say out loud.

"I hope we don't have damage from this storm." It was nice to have her three sisters with her. When Becca married and moved to live with Saul, the sisters had all moved to share this bedroom. That way the boys could spread out. Before, Dinah had shared a room with only Becca, while Naomi and Faith had the other.

When Abby had moved back—the farm she'd lived on with Gabe having been sold—and the three older sisters had shared a room until Becca married.

On the roof now, Dinah heard the drumming rain, with flashes of lightning showing at the window. She found herself counting the seconds between the lightning and the rolling, crashing thunder that followed to realize these happened at almost the same time. The storm was directly overhead.

The wind howled at the window, shrieking and moaning past the glass panes.

Closing her eyes, Dinah focused on the pounding of the rain outside. This was usually a peaceful, lovely sound, a gift from *Gott* to nourish the ground.

The power of it tonight, though, seemed anything but a gift and she knew that damage had to be done. She wondered if there would be trees lost to this, hoping that other families were safe and snug in their beds.

The wild animals would be tucked under leaves and branches, snug in burrows and holes in tree trunks. She had no idea where the birds went when the weather was like this, but she knew they were protected.

The *Haus* shuddered then as another buffet of wind shook it.

"What was that?" Faith said, having startled awake..

"It's just rain," Abby said in a matter-of-fact voice.

Dinah didn't say anything, too busy sending up prayers for *Gott* to be with them. This was silly, of course, as she knew He was always with them, but still…

"I don't think I've ever felt the *Haus* shake like this." At that moment, Faith sounded much younger than her fourteen years.

"We're all together," Dinah said, trying to reassure herself, as well as, her youngest sister.

"This is a strong *Haus*," Abigail said. "*Daed* and our neighbors built it strong. We've weathered harder storms. You just don't remember them."

Dinah didn't remember any this loud, but there had been big storms over the years.

Another crash of thunder had her sending up another prayer for them all to be safe.

The next morning, Dinah woke to the sounds of her younger sisters chatting quietly as they dressed for the day. Abby wasn't there and her bed was made, neat as a pin.

Dinah squinted at the sunlight streaming through the window, as cheerful as if storms hadn't rolled through during the night.

"*Goedemorgen*," she offered in a sleep-husky voice. "What time is it?"

"Time for you to get up," Naomi quipped. "*Mamm* just called up that Abby has breakfast ready."

"She does?" Levering herself up in her bed, Dinah rubbed her eyes. "I guess that storm had us all awake last night."

"It was crazy," Faith said, the look on her young face both troubled and filled with awe. "*Daed* said some boards were blown off the barn and a few shingles of the roof off the *Haus*. Everything not tied down in the backyard and the corral by the barn was all tossed around."

"It's a blessing that we didn't have more damage," Dinah commented. "The winds were violent. I felt the *Haus* shudder."

"Come on down to breakfast," Naomi recommended. "I'm sure the hens and other animals need to be fed. We just need to go on."

"I hope the hen house wasn't blown to bits," Dinah commented.

Having gotten out of bed and reached for the clothes on the peg by her bed, she reflected that Naomi was growing each day more like Abby, different in that she was more open. Bossy, but more bright and cheerful.

Downstairs, *Mamm* stirred a pot on the stove, while Naomi set another bowl at the table. Only her two youngest brothers, Noah and Ezra, sat at the table with Faith.

Sitting down at the table at the chair where Naomi had set her place, Dinah asked, "Have *Daed* and the other boys gone out?"

"*Yah*," Abby said, just having come in with a basket of eggs. "The hen *Haus* is okay, but several boards were blown off the side of the barn."

"Is the barn roof okay? Faith asked.

"It is," responded her oldest sister. "Some shingles were taken off the roof of the *Haus*, but it isn't very bad.

Dinah stirred the hot cereal in her bowl.

"They're still looking over the roof," Abby added, "but Judah just came back from getting the supplies needed to fix the barn wall and he said that several others at the store had terrible losses. I believe the Eberly barn is heavily damaged. Judah also said that Levi Becker was at the hardware, buying glass for his shop's big front window. The storm blew it out and jumbled stuff all around.

Everything got soaked from the rain. The Reese's lost a big part of their *Haus'* roof. Thank *Gott*, they're all fine."

"Levi?" Dinah put down her spoon. "The shop was messed up?"

"Apparently." Abby set her egg basket on the counter near the stove. "Judah said Levi told him everything in the store was moved and shoved around, blown by the storm. Some toys were ruined and Judah said some of the shingles blew off the roof. Rain came in a hole there."

Dinah jolted up from the table. "Oh! My goodness! I need to go!"

"Now?" Faith said, her voice startled. "Before breakfast? On Sunday!"

Mamm turned from the stove to look at her. "You don't work on Sunday."

"Levi will need help no matter what the day." Dinah glanced at her bowl, bending to shovel in several bites. "I have to go. He needs me."

Later that morning, Levi stood back to examine the new pane of glass he'd just installed. It looked level and well caulked.

He knew that the inside of the shop had been trashed by the storm, but that had to wait.

Hearing footsteps approaching, he looked around to face the parking lot. To his shock, Dinah Zook marched right past him without a word, going through the open shop door.

"What are you doing here?" he called out, talking to her through the new window glass. "It's Sunday. Why aren't you with your *familye*?"

A broom already in her hand, she came to the window, looking at him as if he were crazy.

"Our *Haus* wasn't hit like the shop," she said.

Then, as if she'd said all that needed to be said, she went back to shoveling wet, ruined toys toward the door.

"But it's a Sunday," he repeated, having gone to the shop's open door.

She looked at him with lifted brows. "I know the day. Surely, you're used to neighbors helping? Where are your sisters?"

Swallowing a sudden lump in his throat, Levi said, "*Yah,* I suppose neighbors help. My sisters are all working on their farms. The two that live in the area, anyway."

"If you're used to your neighbors helping, then my being here shouldn't be a surprise," she said as she gathered several damp dolls into a basket. "I'll hang these from the porch rails to see if they're salvageable."

He stared as Dinah disappeared into the back room.

As Levi knew, family helped family and friends did help friends. Building houses and barns for one another was an annual ritual. He shouldn't be surprised at her being here to help, but he was.

When she came back to the shop showroom, he said, "The storm was very strong. It had to have done some damage to your farm. My friends are coming to help, but they must do this later, as their own homes require work."

"Our *Haus* and barn also lost a few shingles, but my *Daed* and *Bruders* are working to repair the damage," she said almost cheerfully. "What else needs to be done here?"

"I cleaned up the limbs around the shop before I started on the window. You must be needed at home to clean up your farm." He still felt a little dazed that she'd come.

She squinted a little at him, shaking her head. "It's almost like you don't want my help."

Levi didn't answer right away, stepping several feet away to place in a nearby tool bucket the rag he'd used to clean the caulk off his fingers. Stepping back to the shop doorway, he said in a husky tone, "I do want your help."

"Good," she said in a matter-of-fact voice, "I'd hate to think I am bothering you."

"No, of course not."

The shop was a mess with kick scooters piled together beside one wall and water all over the floor, no doubt from rain blown in at the broken windows. He'd already fixed the large front window, but a smaller one on the side of the building had also been broken, a large tree branch having crashed into it. Sadly, the hardware store was out of glass to fit this one.

After they'd swept out the water and set the scooters out to dry in the now-cheerful sunlight, Levi said, "Can you come hold this board over the window? I need to nail it shut, until I can get glass for it."

"Sure." She'd been wiping the counter after collecting several smaller branches and twigs from around the shop.

She followed him out of the building, coming around to the side. The broken window was higher than the one at the front of the shop. While he pulled the branch out of the opening, throwing it aside, Dinah waited, holding his hammer and a bucket of nails that she'd collected from his tool bucket on the front porch.

"Just let me get these glass shards out first."

"Okay."

Levi tugged several jagged pieces of the window loose, brushing aside the smaller ones with a gloved hand. "Careful with those!"

In the process of loading the glass he'd pulled from the window frame into a smaller bucket, she threw him a grin. "Don't worry. I've worked with my *Daed* for years. This isn't the first time I've picked up pieces of glass."

He turned back to the gaping hole in the wall. "Good."

Laboring alongside her felt weird…and right, at the same time. Probably, he concluded, because they worked beside one another in the shop, just not like this.

"Here." Lifting the plywood square that he'd bought from the hardware, Levi positioned it over the window. "Hold it while I nail."

Dinah shifted around to press the board firmly over the gaping window, while he took nails from the bucket she'd brought round from the porch. He put several of these in his mouth and reached over her shoulder to hammer one in at a top corner, setting the nail with a determined whack.

It was a stretch to reach over her and carefully do this, but thankfully, he was tall enough to make the stretch. Midway through this, though, her clean, fresh scent wafted up to him—not surprising as they were nearly touching—and Levi swallowed hard. He could feel the warmth of her body…and this really wasn't good. It felt too good. He didn't want to notice Dinah's body or her clean smell.

He'd been trying not to notice her, at least, not in this way. She worked for him and he'd offered to help her sort through the *Menner* in her life. Noticing her made her seem too close.

He was determined not to risk again the pain he'd felt after losing his wife and child.

Levi tucked the hammer under one arm to free a hand to scratch his eyebrow, mumbling, "Sorry."

"Not a problem." She sounded a little breathless herself and he shifted to reach around her other side to nail in the lower corner.

Pausing for a moment, nearly wrapped around Dinah, he filled his lungs with her scent, knowing he shouldn't. He definitely shouldn't stand here so close to her.

They neither said a word, just frozen in that position. She gave a small gasp and Levi realized his own breath was a little jagged.

Jolting himself into action, he shifted a foot back, reaching up to slam in—with unnecessary force—a nail into the other top corner. He quickly moved to hammer in the one remaining corner of the board before stepping completely away from her.

The few minutes after, neither said a word…and Levi prayed to *Gott* to protect him from this danger.

CHAPTER SEVEN

Four days later, Dinah, crouched before a lower shelf, arranging the little faceless dolls she'd washed and dried after the storm mess.

The shop had been filled with *Kinder* all afternoon, as school was on spring holidays, but they'd all left and, for the first time, no one was there, but Levi and Dinah.

He broke the silence that had fallen over the shop. "Did I ever thank you?"

In the days before this—and after the storm—he hadn't said much, at all.

She turned to look at him. "For what?"

He took a breath. "For coming to help clean this place up. I know I haven't always been your favorite person."

A little glow spread through her midsection at his acknowledgement. "You're welcome, but I'm sure your friends would have come to help eventually."

"*Yah*, they would and neighbors, too, I know. It's just that you came right away. Left your *familye* to clean up your own place and came to help here."

She smiled at him, not really sure what to say. Levi seemed…friendlier these days. He seemed nicer the longer she worked with him. After she'd talked about Bart and her difficulties knowing how to trust another *Mann*.

Silence descended again and they both went back to their work. She knew she needed to go to the back room to wash some more toys, but for whatever reason, this didn't seem important right now.

"I don't think I've ever told you about Anna, my wife."

Looking up at his words, Dinah said after a moment of surprise, "Only that you loved her."

"I did love her. Very much." He wiped a cloth over another kick scooter before adding. "This may seem strange to you."

She might not be ready to completely absolve him of deliberately hurting Abby, even if he'd offered that terse apology, but she said, "I do know that you've had a rough go of it."

It was the truth. To have lost a wife had to have been difficult.

Nodding, he said, "Even though, it's been a while now, I still—still think of her sometimes."

With a short, soft laugh, Dinah said, "Of course, you do. That's natural. I know Abby still thinks of Gabe, and he's been gone for some time."

"The bishop has been after me to marry again," Levi said abruptly. "That's why I suggested we marry. I'm sorry about having suggested a loveless union to you."

"That did surprise me," she said, "especially after what you said about Abby. Don't most *Menner* want wives to give them lots of *Kinder*? If only to work on their farms. If you thought my sister withheld this from Gabe, I would think you'd wonder if I would, too."

"I don't think Abby withheld children from Gabe. I was, I guess, upset about my own loss. I suggested that you and I marry without love and I don't want love again. It's too much risk, but…" He looked down again to the scooter in his hands, "you deserve better."

"*Denki*. So do you, actually. Not more loss." After a few minutes of silence, Dinah took a deep breath, plunging into speech. "If you don't mind my asking, how did Anna die?'

Levi sent her a long look, seeming to assess whether he wanted to answer the question. "She died—she died while having our child. The baby died, too. Grace."

The words came out with little expression and the very blankness of his face made his loss seem more painful. He'd obviously known deep sorrow.

"Oh!" She didn't know what she'd expected, but this certainly wasn't it. "I'm so sorry. I shouldn't have asked."

"You couldn't have known," he said, his voice matching his lack of expression. "I'm sure my *familye* hasn't said much—if anything—about it. I don't talk about it myself."

Dinah's chest felt tight and she didn't know what to say. Maybe losing a child along with his wife had made him say what he'd said about Gabe not having children.

Levi shrugged. "Time has passed."

Not able to keep from words tumbling out, she said, "Yet, you haven't found a *Maedel* to love? Even with the bishop prodding you?"

His lip curled cynically. "*Neh.* Like I said, I don't think I want to risk that again and I don't think the bishop was concerned with whether or not I found a *Maedel* to love. Just that I married and started a family. Besides, I'm not sure—"

"What?" she asked, swinging around to look at him more fully. "What did you start to say?"

Moving to place the now-clean scooter against the wall by the front window, Levi shrugged again. "It doesn't matter. I just don't feel inclined to court any of the girls here."

Wanting to ask him if he felt inclined to look elsewhere to find a girl he liked, Dinah pressed her lips together to keep the words inside. She'd never blurted out her thoughts before. Becca was the impulsive one. Keeping her thoughts to herself, Dinah reflected that others had certainly secured marriage brokers—or matchmakers—to find mates.

Still, she didn't need to say anything about this!

"If you don't marry again, how will you ever have more *Bopplin*?" A little appalled at herself, Dinah pressed her lips shut again. Whatever was the matter with her!

Slowly, he responded. "I'm not sure I'm ready to do that again, either."

"You aren't?" She couldn't keep the surprise out of her voice.

He replied slowly, "What you love can be lost."

"Oh."

After his mean comment about Abby, Dinah hadn't thought she'd ever feel sympathy towards Levi, but she registered then that she'd been wrong.

The next Sunday, Levi sat under a tree with his friend, Reuben, the two eating from the plates of food from the lunch after their meeting.

"You had a lot of damage from the storm? It caused a mess for most." Levi chewed for a moment, the thoughts that had been circling in his head for a week, still not clear. They were troubling, however.

Flashing back to the electric moment when he'd hovered over Dinah Zook to nail the board over the shop window, he felt again the blossoming of warmth in his chest. This wouldn't do.

"You said the shop window blew out?" Reuben asked. "That must have made a mess."

Still chewing—and wondering if he should talk about that moment with Dinah—Levi said, "*Yah*, it did. Things inside were drenched and thrown about. I got a pane of glass for the big window up front, but Jeb, at the hardware, was out of glass for the back window by the time I got to the store."

"I'm sorry I couldn't come help. Rachel and I worked all day to replace roof shingles and the *Kinder* helped clean up the small tree limbs in the yard."

"Even little Eli? He's still in a cradle!"

"Well, *neh*, not Eli, but Zach toddled around in the yard, helping do his best."

"Must have been difficult for Rachel to help with the roof, when she had to watch the children."

"It was. Her brother, John, did help after he took care of what his farm needed. He wasn't hit as bad as most. I'm sorry to have left you to repair the damage to your shop alone."

"I didn't do it all on my own. Simon and Aaron came to help after they repaired their own places…and Dinah was a big help."

Levi didn't know why he'd thrown that in. It was true, though, and his thoughts had been twisting over her more and more. It couldn't be. He hadn't felt anything towards any woman since Anna and he didn't want to go there ever again, no matter if the bishop kept pushing.

"Dinah Zook?"

He looked up at his friend. "*Yah.*"

"You've said she's doing a good job, but she came on a Sunday to help? Wasn't she needed at her own family's farm?"

"*Neh,* not from what she said." He took another bite, not sure he should even talk about the stuff swirling in his head.

"Oh." Reuben didn't say anything more.

Feeling spurred to speak, Levi confessed, "She bothers me."

"What do you mean? Doesn't she work as well as you thought?"

"She works very well," admitted Levi in a frustrated voice.

Reuben said slowly, "Then what bothers you?"

Not able to voice a complete, rational response to this, he exclaimed, "She smells good!"

"Oh." From his friend's expression, Reuben saw the problem in this.

Levi set his half-empty plate on the ground next to him.

"Maybe you could avoid getting too close to her."

"She also hums when she works and, did you hear what I said? She came on a Sunday just to help me!"

"I heard. I heard." Reuben put down his own plate.

"And then when I asked her to hold the board I had to put over the back window—" Levi stopped, afraid to even voice the moment. "I—"

"You smelled her again," his friend concluded in a morose voice.

"Yes, I did…and then, the next day, I told her about Anna and the baby dying."

Reuben turned to stare at him. "You did? You haven't even told me about that."

Nodding, Levi said, "I know, but I told her."

Reuben grimaced. "You could fire her. That way you wouldn't have to smell her."

The thought of only seeing Dinah at the meetings every other week made Levi say, "What reason could I give for that?"

Shaking his head, his friend said, "I don't know. Even though, you thought you could manage on your own, after Esther married, you've only said Dinah being there makes things at the shop better."

"I know." The pressure in his chest got heavier. "I can't do it again, Reuben. I can't."

Reuben raised his brows, nodding in understanding. "Some in the church never marry. They devote themselves to tilling the land and caring for their parents.

"You know that my *Eldre* have gone to live with Mary and Thomas, right?"

"*Yah*, I do know that, but they could come live here or you could just not marry."

Levi heaved a big sigh.

"Or—hear me out, now—you could marry a woman you don't love. Just one you tolerate." His friend looked to be in the throes of having a great, new idea. "You know. One that wouldn't—what did you say after Anna died—tear your insides out?"

Reuben looked so enamored of his idea that Levi hated to mention that he'd already tried that…with Dinah.

"That wouldn't be very kind to the *Maedel*," he responded. He'd learned something from his failed proposal to her.

"Maybe not," Reuben admitted, "but you could choose an older, plain girl."

"You mean a desperate girl? It still wouldn't be kind to take that kind of step and not tell her."

"No," his friend said doubtfully, "but the *Maedel* still might say yes."

"Maybe," Levi said finally, getting up. "I'll think about it. Here, I'll take our plates back to be washed."

Even if he could find such a woman, it still wouldn't keep him from remembering that breathless moment when his arms had been around Dinah.

A week later, Dinah worked up the courage to mention her dilemma to Abby while the two of them were hanging garments on the clothesline. She hated that all her buggy drives with all the different *Menner* had yielded her only more frustration and confusion, but she couldn't keep denying it to herself.

And then there was her accepting Levi's help with this. She'd told no one about this and found herself more comfortable talking about the struggle with Levi than with anyone, even her *familye*. She didn't want to ponder what that meant.

"Abby," she stumbled into speech, keeping her voice low as not to draw her younger sisters' attention, weeding in the nearby kitchen garden.

"What?" Abby was neat as a pin despite the growing warmth of the day. She usually looked completely neat, with her white *Kapp* a perfect frame for her fair complexion.

Dinah hesitated a moment. "I keep driving out with different *Menner*. I just—I just.... I don't know."

"You sound troubled," Abby said after Dinah's voice trailed off.

"Are you still okay with me working for Levi? You'd tell me if you were not, yes?"

"Yes, I would. You know I don't mind that you're working with him. You said he apologized for his words. He and I both lost mates. I can understand that he was upset."

"And his coolness and unfriendliness to others?" Dinah asked. "It's amazing that he has any business!"

"You did say" her sister reminded her, "that he's always friendly to the children who come to his shop and he's gotten friendly with you."

"*Yah*. Yes, he is kindly toward the *Kinder*." Trying to maintain her irritation, Dinah said, "He probably knows he needs them to make a living."

"Sister," Abby chided. "He didn't have to build a business that appealed to children. He likes them. He just doesn't have any."

Dinah clipped her pin over the fabric of one of her brothers' coats on the clothesline. For whatever reason—and she didn't care to examine this too closely—she'd never told anyone about Levi's proposal. He hadn't meant it, she thought now. Not really.

"How am I to know which *Mann* is to be more trustworthy than Bart?" she asked abruptly. "I drive out with different ones, but—none seem right. Clearly more reliable, I mean."

Abby lifted her brows. "I understand. It seems like you will just know, but you've certainly seen a number. None seem better."

"That's the problem," Dinah said irritably, readjusting a pair of pants to hang better on the line. "They all seem better, just not…."

"Right?"

"That's what I mean." She frowned at her sister. "I was wrong before. What's to say I won't be wrong again?"

Abby pinned a shirt to the line by the shoulders. "Perhaps rely on *Gott*? He is our best guidance. After all, He did save you from marriage to Bart."

That next Sunday evening, *crack!!* went the bat in Dinah's hand and she flung it aside to race toward first base. Off to the side—in the space her team waited—was hooting and yelling for the hit. She could hear Levi's voice above the others and told herself, pounding toward the base, to get a grip.

It didn't do any good, she reflected as she stood panting on the base, to be so aware of him.

All her brothers and sisters were there that afternoon and she heard Faith cheering for her, even though her youngest sister was on the other team.

"Woohoo, Dinah!

She saw Levi up to bat and realized the batting order must have been changed and now he followed her.

The ball was pitched and Levi let it pass. When the pitcher threw the next, Dinah tensed, leaning forward to bound off the base as she watched the white orb sail up in the air and come right down in the strike zone.

When Levi's bat hit the ball, Dinah streaked forward, headed to the next base.

The rest of the game passed in a blur until the other team won by one run.

Walking up the small incline to the *Haus*, she saw that Levi had come up next to her. With a smile that seemed almost conspiratorial, he said, "We'll get them next time."

Later that evening, Dinah sat next to her friend, Mary Reese. The singing was now over and most others were gathered around the tables that held food.

"How are things going with Aaron?"

The two sat alone and Mary gave a dimpled smile before saying in a lowered voice, "I know I can tell you without you thinking I'm bragging—Aaron has asked me to be his wife."

Dinah blinked before rousing herself. "Mary! That is wonderful."

This wasn't a surprise, but it did put right in Dinah's face that she was to have been married by this time and couldn't now decide on a *Mann*.

"*Denki*." Mary smiled, looking very pleased.

"How lovely for you both!"

She kept her voice lowered in her congratulations as these matters were considered private. "Not that this is a surprise. Aaron has been *narrish* over you since the two of you were in school."

Mary gave a soft laugh. "He's no more crazy over me than I am over him."

They both looked across the room at where Aaron talked with several other *Menner*. Levi was part of the group and another *Mann*—Joel Woomart—who Dinah hadn't seen for a while. If she remembered, he'd been away, helping some relatives establish themselves on a new farm.

Still in lowered tones, she said, "How wonderful that Aaron proposed now. This way you can marry in the fall and your *Mamm* will still be able to plant vegetables for the meal."

"*Yah*," Mary said with a happy sigh.

Dinah swung a quick glance her way. "You don't mind that Aaron doesn't have a place of his own yet?"

"Of course not. We'll live with John, his older brother, and Sarah, at first. Aaron thinks we'll be able to afford some land of our own in five years. You know, Sarah is so cheerful and friendly. I'm sure living with John and her will be lovely. She'll be glad to have help with their young *familye*, too."

Her friend chattered on happily, her life spreading out before her, like a settled, pleasing path.

Dinah couldn't help thinking that she, just like Mary, had thought her life was falling into place—a *Mann* who loved her, marriage and children. Now, she was stuck, living with her own *familye* still and unable to know which *Mann* to pick.

Sometime later, she stood by the table loaded with desserts when Joel Woomert himself came up to her.

"Dinah!" He smiled at her. "How are you doing?"

Holding a plate with several desserts, she responded. "I am well."

"And your *familye*? I've been gone so long, I feel I must meet everyone again!"

She flapped a hand at him. "It's not been that long. You were helping your cousin set up his new farm, yes?"

"I was. Cousin Jeremiah. He and his wife just bought a farm a hundred miles north of here and I helped them move in. There was much to be done."

"I understand he needed a new barn, as well."

"*Yah.*" Joel looked around the big room at the Wissler *Haus*. "This is certainly a well-attended Sing."

Dinah bit back a smile at his observation. All the Sings in Fairfield County were well-attended. "It is."

"I'm so glad to be able to see so many of our friends."

"Yes."

Joel gave her another cheerful smile. "Would you let me drive you home tonight?"

His cheerful tone made him seem even more attractive.

"Okay," she responded, even more mindful of her search for a trustworthy *Mann*. Levi's offer to help her sort all this out made her feel less alone in the hunt.

CHAPTER EIGHT

"Then," Dinah told Levi the next Monday, "Joel Woomert asked to drive me home from the last Sing."

"Joel?" Levi mused, pausing in putting together another scooter. "He just came back to town, didn't he?"

They both sat at the tall counter in the store, the front door opened to allow in the fresh morning breeze.

"*Yah*. He was north of here, helping a cousin set up his new farm."

"And how did the drive go? Can you see yourself trusting him?" Levi waited.

"I don't know." She was quiet for a moment, apparently considering the question.

"I don't know him well." Levi couldn't say why her dilemma drew his interest, but he understood how this was a difficult choice. "He was behind me in school, but our classroom wasn't big, as you know. Joel always seemed decent then."

"So did Bart," she countered in a gloomy voice, "in some ways."

"*Yah*, that's true, but *Gott* is with you. Maybe it's His blessing that you didn't end up marrying Bart." Levi polished the scooter footboard in his hand.

"Maybe. I just wished *Gott* had given me a clue earlier."

Shrugging, Levi said, "Perhaps He did. It can be hard to hear His voice."

"I'm listening as hard as I can now." On her perch on a stool several feet away, she responded with a shrug of her own. "I wish

I'd get a really sign. A light overhead shining directly over the right *Mann*."

"It doesn't work that way," Levi commented. "We are given heart signals, I think. You're supposed to know inside."

"I don't know." The gloomy note was back in her voice. "Joel seemed nice, but a lot of *Menner* seem that way. Bart seemed nice. I just can't tell who is not like Bart."

"Maybe," he suggested, "you're just afraid. That can block judgment."

She turned, staring at him, "What do you mean?

He shrugged again. As odd as the conversation was, Levi felt comfortable talking with her like this. "Scared. The situation with Bart has made you doubt yourself. Seems like it's colored your thoughts about all the *Menner* you've considered."

"That's what *Grossmammie* Ruth said," Dinah admitted. "Maybe you're both right. I am afraid of making the wrong choice again. I fear making the same mistake. I don't know how to change this, though."

Levi hesitated for a moment. He'd talked a lot to *Gott* since Anna died. "Maybe you should pray."

"I do that all the time."

"Maybe you need to pray to *Gott* to do what He thinks best. That's what you want, isn't it? Don't you think *Gott* wants you to do the best for you? And maybe you need to trust yourself? You have learned from this, haven't you?"

She sat silently for a moment before saying impulsively, "Maybe you should pray, too. Ask *Gott* to give you another love and not fear another loss."

Levi shook his head. "I'm not letting that happen. I told you. I'll marry a *Maedel* who isn't concerned with being loved. You don't have to worry about that, though. Remember, you're looking for a *Mann* to trust…and you hope this next one is the one."

"Yes, I have hope." Dinah smiled. "It's nice to be able to talk about this. My *familye* all have opinions and it's hard to see through those."

He grinned at her. "You're welcome."

Levi was right, Dinah thought later that evening. She did need to ask *Gott* for the best outcome. After all, *Gott* only wanted the best for her and He was so great, He could see what she couldn't.

The kitchen was silent now, her *Grossmammie* at the stove, stirring the evening's stew while Dinah's mother took a pan of roasted beets and potatoes—left over from last year's harvest—from the oven.

Dinah paused in setting the table. "How did you know? Both of you, I mean. How did you know you were marrying the right *Menner*?"

She'd been praying on and off all day, since talking with Levi, and now it occurred to her that she could use the knowledge of her own *familye* to help her. Smiling at the thought that *Gott* had inserted the realization into her head, Dinah waited for the women's response.

Her *Mamm* looked up from the baking pan. "Oh! That is a surprising question."

"You have an answer, don't you?"

Seeming to ponder the matter, Mary Zook smiled. "Like you, I had many *Menner* want to court with me."

"I hope none were as fickle as Bart," Dinah muttered.

"*Neh*, but none except your *Daed* felt…right."

"That's it? He felt right?" This made no sense to her.

"Your *Grossdaddi* and I didn't get along, at all."

Swiveling around at these unexpected words from her grandmother, Dinah stared.

Her *Grossmammi* Ruth looked over her shoulder with a funny expression. "He annoyed me like fire."

"What?"

"You never said that," Dinah's mother said mildly. "I always thought the two of you got along very well."

Grossmammi laughed. "We did, of course, by the time we met you. Not at first, of course. We had such fights! Then we learned to really see each other. To listen. I loved him very much. Still do."

"But you didn't love him initially?" This still seemed a confusing thing to Dinah. "Then why did you court with him?"

Her grandmother came away from the stove, setting the pot of stew on a hot pad on the table. "I didn't when I first knew him. He seemed braggy and too sure of himself. When he first came to work, building my family's new barn—our old one burned, you know—I didn't like him."

Startled at the view of her grandparents' history, Dinah could only drop into a seat at the table and stare at the older woman.

"You must have come to see him differently?"

Abigail came into the kitchen then, getting herself a cup of coffee from the pot on the stove.

"Oh, yes," *Grossmammi* continued. "Not right away, but after a while."

"What changed your mind about him?" This could be helpful, mused Dinah.

"What are they talking about?" Abby asked their *Mamm* in a lowered voice.

"How Ruth came to love *Grossdaddi* John," *Mamm* answered.

"Oh." Abby clearly still didn't get the direction of the conversation.

"Over time, I came to see that he did know a lot—about barn building and other things."

"You don't marry a Mann because he knows how to build a barn," her mother commented with a smile.

Grossmammi laughed again. "Your grandfather didn't seem friendly and he was very bossy."

Levi's image flashed in Dinah's mind, leaving her frowning. She'd loved her *Grossdaddi* very much, remembering him playing with her brothers and sisters and teasing them when they grew older. Oddly, she could see Levi—but not necessarily Joel—doing this.

She screwed up her face. "You didn't like *Grossdaddi*? He was so wonderful."

"Yes," her mother confirmed. "He was by the time you knew him, but I do remember that he was quiet when I first got to know him."

"By that time," her grandmother confirmed in a dry voice. "He'd learned not to look so stern with strangers."

"He did play a lot with you grandchildren. All his grandchildren, really."

"And he didn't seem this way in the beginning?" Dinah's memory of her grandfather was loving and wonderful. It was hard to see him having been different.

Grossmammi Ruth chuckled. "I hope we all learn as we grow older. He was different before we married. At least, with me. Your grandfather played with his own children quite a lot."

"How did he change? Why didn't you like him, at first?"

Her grandmother sent her a dry look. "He was bossy and snappy with me and he acted like I could do nothing right."

"Oh."

Grossmammi Ruth went on. "Back then, he didn't seem to even notice *Kinder*. He seemed unfriendly and not nice."

"Oh," Dinah said again. "I guess I can see why you didn't like him."

"Well, it wasn't that I didn't like him." Her grandmother took a sip from the cup that her *Mamm* had put in front of the older woman. "I didn't want to like him, but every now and then he'd say something really funny and I had to laugh."

Abby laughed then, seeming to understand.

The corners of Dinah's mouth lifted. She remembered this—her grandfather making her grandmother laugh—even when they were both old.

"How did *Grossdaddi* learn to change the things that bothered you?"

"I told him straight out when he needed it! He worked on my *Daed's* farm, then."

At her grandmother's astringent tone, Dinah smiled. She made it sound so simple. "And when did you know that *Grossdaddi* was the *Mann* for you?"

"I suppose," her grandmother mused, "it was when I saw that he was listening to me. You know, making changes I suggested. After a while, I started to warm to him. I realized that he had started to matter to me."

Dinah looked down at the tabletop. She guessed that was the issue. She didn't feel she mattered to the *Menner* who took her driving. Not really. Sure, they were clearly interested, but did she actually matter to any of them?

Sitting at the shop counter a week later, Dinah counted the sales reflected in the ledger as Levi spoke to several children at the other end of the counter.

When these boys had left, silence descended over the shop until Dinah thought to look up from her work.

"I meant to tell you, I saw Joel speaking to two *Youngies* at the meeting last Sunday. He suggested one *Buwe* accept Joel driving him to the *Buwe's* home. Wasn't that nice of him?"

Looking over from putting away a kick scooter that he'd shown to his customers, Levi said, "*Yah*, I suppose."

"What do you mean, you suppose?" she exclaimed.

Levi shrugged. "Did Joel drive out of his way? Taking the *Buwe* to a *Haus* on the way to Joel's wasn't that big a deal."

"It was," she insisted. "He didn't have to drive the boy, at all!"

"If I remember right," Levi said in a dry tone, "Joel is very out-going. Give a *Kinder* a buggy ride home would give Joel someone to talk to."

"You have no right to say that!" Being honest with herself, she had to admit that she'd been excited to see this kindness in a *Mann* to whom she hoped she'd get attached. Levi's observations irritated her, though.

"Maybe it was kind of Joel." Levi's voice was mild. "Since he's younger than me, we didn't spend much time together at school."

Just then, Dinah's sisters came through the shop's open front doors.

"Becca!" she cried, slipping down from her tall stool to come around the counter to hug her sister. "I know I've said this before, but the black *Kapp* looks wonderful on you."

"Becca has news," Faith teased, "and we came to tell you."

"Shhh," her sister said. "You know this isn't to be bragged about."

Since Saul and Becca had been married for almost a year now, Dinah had a suspicion what her younger sister referred to. "How are things going? We haven't seen you for several weeks since you didn't come to the sermon last Sunday. *Mamm* said Saul told her you felt bad."

"I wonder why," Faith teased pertly.

"Hush, *Youngie*," Abby admonished as Becca blushed. "We should have left you home. Are you even old enough to have finished school?"

"I am now," Faith confirmed, clearly not embarrassed.

"Sorry, *Mamm* made us bring her," Naomi said, grimacing at Dinah.

She smiled, not mentioning the nuisance Naomi had made of herself in younger years when sent on various errands with Abby, Dinah and Becca.

"I hope you're feeling better."

"It comes and goes, she said," Naomi commented, joining her younger sister in making teasing remarks.

"I'm fine," Becca said, giving her sisters an admonishing look. "*Hallo* Levi. How are you?"

"I'm fine, as well," he replied, grinning. Most likely at the sisters' interaction.

"Good. And business in your shop is going well?" Becca plowed forward, acting as if her two younger sisters—now giggling together—didn't exist.

"*Yah*. Dinah helped clean up after that last storm. She was very handy. Did you and Saul get much damage?"

"Some, but not as much as many farms around here. Dinah said the shop was hit hard…"

Listening to Levi and her sister talk, Dinah tried not to wish the girls gone. She wanted to finish the conversation in which she and Levi had been engaged, to ask Levi if he thought Joel wasn't the *Mann* he seemed. His opinion wouldn't remove Joel from her consideration, but she still wanted to hear it.

"So," Abby commented two weeks later as the two of them sat in the family room, stitching on a quilt top, "you've driven out with Joel Woomert four times now. Is he the *Mann* to steal your heart?"

Knowing her *familye* had noted that she'd driven out with this *Mann* more than any others, Dinah wasn't surprised at the question. It was actually amazing that no one else in the family hadn't asked before.

"I don't know," she answered honestly, thrusting her needle into the cotton fabric.

She and Abigail had always been close, but she'd talked to Levi more about Joel than to Abby. Dinah just didn't want to raise hopes in her *familye* if there was no reason. Levi was more removed from this and she, thus, felt more comfortable talking about the situation with him. Levi seemed unmoved.

Of course, they were admonished not to brag about upcoming marriages—or births—but parents and siblings were naturally interested. They paid attention.

"And you have kissed?" Abby teased, relaxed as she snapped the sewing thread with her straight teeth.

Dinah ducked her head, embarrassed to talk about this.

"Maybe. Sort of."

Her sister laughed. "Sort of? Tell me how that works."

Instead of answering this, Dinah looked up from the quilt top. "Tell me, sister, how did you know you wanted to marry Gabe?"

"I liked his kisses," Abigail retorted.

"No, seriously."

Her *Schweschder* paused, the moment between them lengthening. "I knew Gabe a long time. He was Adam's friend first, you remember? And we were thrown together a lot since his friend was spending time with my friend, Hannah Otzinger?"

"*Yah*, I remember her. Didn't she marry and move away?"

"Yes. She and Gabe's friend, Judah Royer, married and then an uncle of his left Judah the uncle's farm. That's why they moved."

Abby went back to stitching, her expression now closed in. Dinah suddenly wished she'd never asked her sister about marrying Gabe. Normally, she wouldn't have, but she was tired of driving out with different *Menner*. She wanted to marry and settle down with a family of her own. Maybe she needed to give Joel a chance to be the right one.

Abby finally drew a deep breath, saying, "Anyway, the more I spent time with Gabe, the more I knew. He made me laugh and he could tease me out of my bad moods."

"Joel kissed me on the cheek and I didn't mind," Dinah said hopefully.

Her sister laughed. "That's something, I guess. You'll have to see how it goes from here."

"I will," Dinah said. "Levi said the same thing."

CHAPTER NINE

A week later, Levi stood outside his shop, watching little Jakob Ruffner sailing away on a kick scooter that Levi had just taught him to ride. Levi smiled. He'd started this shop, soon after moving home, looking to make his living doing something he loved and he loved watching little faces light up.

"Hey, you!"

Turning toward the shop's open door, he saw Joel Woomert standing on the shop's porch, an irritated expression on his face.

"*Yah*?"

"I've been standing here several minutes," Joel snapped arrogantly. "Can I get some help?"

"I'm sorry," Levi responded slowly. "My—assistant—should be inside and can help with anything you need."

He didn't want to name Dinah, although he knew Joel knew her and probably knew she worked here.

"No one is here to help me," Joel said with the same irritation. "That's my point."

"Oh." Levi glanced at the open door. "She must have stepped out the back for some reason."

Joel lifted patronizing eyebrows. "Maybe that's why I've not yet been helped."

Glancing down the road to see that Jakob was now riding back toward the shop, Levi said, "Let's go into the shop and I'll see if I can help."

"Good." Joel Woomert went through the door. "I would hope not to wait any longer."

Levi followed the *Mann* in, finding himself hoping that Dinah didn't come back inside. Joel's attitude didn't show him in a good light.

After Joel had bought an item or two, Levi considered the situation. The last few minutes hadn't revealed anything good about Joel. Of course, everyone had bad days and this might have been one of Joel's. Or he might just be a jerk. Either way, Levi decided he wouldn't tell Dinah anything about this. Maybe he should, but she already didn't trust her own judgment. She needed to decide for herself if Joel was a good *Mann*.

Although, he realized that he hated the idea of Dinah with such a skunk.

The next Saturday, Dinah clung to her buggy seat as Joel made a left turn.

"I'm glad you could drive out today," he said, sending her a sideways glance. "You look pretty today."

Uneasily wishing as several other buggies drove past, that he'd keep his eyes on the road, Dinah said, "*Denki*."

Her *familye* and the other *Menner* she'd driven out with hadn't complimented her very often and she wasn't sure how to take it. Joel seemed a little free with his words.

"It is a nice day," she commented, remembering the things that her sister, *Grossmammi* and *Mamm* had said about recognizing love. Of course, not everyone was the same. Dinah tried her best to clear her mind and shake lose the anxiety that she'd again have to deal with another Bart.

She'd thought he'd loved her, until he announced that he was marrying another woman.

"*Yah*," Joel said in a sunny tone. "It has warmed up nicely. Have you and your sisters been busy helping your *Mamm* with the *Haus* and kitchen garden?"

"Yes, of course."

"My sisters, as well."

They whizzed past several other buggies and then an *Englischer* car sailed past them.

Dinah pushed out of her mind every thought of how many *Amische* had been killed or injured in buggy accidents and accidents with cars. In her thoughts about the best husband material, she hadn't listed good buggy driving as very important.

Maybe she should have.

"I wanted to ask you, Dinah," Joel sent her what seemed like an ingratiating smile, "if you'll drive out only with—with me."

His words echoed in her head and she didn't immediately answer him.

They trotted quickly around a slower buggy, which gave her another few minutes to consider her response.

"I realize," he said in a hurried voice, "that you've driven out with a lot of *Menner*, but I'm hoping that you think—as I do—that we get along well. Will you drive out with only me?"

It hit Dinah then that her anxiety in picking a *Mann* had overshadowed the scandal of Bart's rejection.

"Don't you think we do well together?"

She looked down at the fingers of her two hands knitted together in her dilemma. "I'd like to—to think about it Joel."

The next morning, Levi stood next to her outside the shop window, looking at their new display of toys.

"I think it looks good. Your suggestion of adding those two smaller wooden toys at the front balances the display very well."

The early summer sun was warm on her back, the two of them standing in front of the window. She bracketed her hand on her hips, trying not to beam at his comment, although she did feel a strong sense of satisfaction. Dinah hoped this wasn't pride—which she knew wasn't good.

In honesty, she said, "Your choice of those three scooters is the main focus, though, and I like the way you angled them."

He laughed, patting her shoulder. "We work well together, then."

"We do," she agreed as they turned to head inside.

Levi went over to straighten the scooters along the wall inside. "How has the hunt been going?"

"Hunt?"

He elaborated, "To find an honest, trustworthy *Mann*."

Dinah looked down at the planked floor. "*Gut*, I think. I'm still looking—and the *Menner* around here seem to think this is a contest of some kind."

"With you as the prize?" Levi teased, coming around the counter to perch on a stool in front of his work bench.

"Apparently so, from something one of them said." She didn't know why, but she felt shy to name the *Mann* who'd said this. She also wasn't ready to talk about Joel's request that she drive out with only him.

"At least, it's better to be thought a prize than to be pitied for Bart's actions."

"Very true," she agreed. "Although, I want a *Mann* looking to do more than win."

Joel's declaration could only mean that he wanted them to court and it seemed early to say after only a few drives. Of course, they knew one another from school and had both lived in this town all their lives, although they'd never had a lot of dealings.

She'd always been with Bart, Dinah reflected.

Picking up a screwdriver to tinker with a scooter wheel from the work bench, Levi lifted his brows, saying, "I don't think it's a bad thing to have a *Mann* want to win you. Don't you want that?"

"*Yah*, of course, but not if he was only trying to be with me because he wants to show up the other *Menner* around here."

"Do you think that's the case?" Levi looked at her, the tool in his hand apparently forgotten. "If I were you, I wouldn't want to drive out with anyone who seemed this way."

"No," she grimaced at him. "I'm still sorting through whether this is the situation."

"Ahh, I understand."

He said this in a relaxed manner and Dinah thought she might have been talking to a girlfriend—or a sister. Levi no longer seemed like the aloof, unfriendly *Mann* who hurt her sister. The change had been coming on slowly. He was the same *Mann*, though.

This was all so confusing.

Later that night, after the *familye* had finished supper and now sat in the living room reading, Dinah stood at the kitchen sink with Abby. Naomi's laugh rang out in the other room and she heard Faith utter a protesting sputter as the two played at some game.

"Abby?"

"Hmm?" Her older sister handed her a soapy dish to rinse.

Launching into speech, Dinah said, "I just don't know what to make of him?"

"Who? Joel Woomert?"

Ironically, Joel's request hadn't been occupying her mind this afternoon. She just kept circling around what she knew of Levi and the friend he'd become.

"*Neh*, Levi."

"What about him?" Abby slid another plate into the water in the sink.

Rinsing the one in her hands, Dinah said, "Have you ever had one opinion of a person and then found them seeming the very opposite?"

Her sister smiled at the sink. "I thought we might not have seen the whole of Levi in that one ugly moment. After all, he was Gabe's good friend."

"Yes, but everyone liked your husband and he liked everyone." Dinah sputtered in frustration at her dilemma. "Gabe was just that kind of a *Mann*. Sweet and forgiving to all."

"He was," Abby agreed. "This is part of the reason I don't expect to ever love another."

"You will. You were—and will be again—a wonderful wife for some *Mann*."

"I won't argue with you about that," Abby said in a calm voice, "but I see no one here."

Momentarily distracted from the thoughts that had been circling in her head, Dinah asked, "Have *Mamm* or *Daed* ever said anything about you marrying again?"

"No, bless them."

"I'm surprised that none of the bishops have urged you to do so. They're probably too afraid."

Abby laughed. "What?"

"Admit it, sister, you can be unapproachable."

Drawing a long breath, her sister said nothing in response to this.

"I'm sure it can be handy. At least, you're not being pestered."

"I think you mean 'counseled' and this is the job that bishops are directed to do."

"Well, they haven't counseled you," Dinah observed. "Anyway, what do you think I should do about Levi?"

"Do about him?" Abby turned to look at her.

"I just don't know what to think," she returned fretfully.

"Maybe you just need to be glad you're seeing him in a better light."

"I guess." Dinah didn't want to say that seeing Levi this way made her uneasy. It was disturbing to like the *Mann* with whom she worked, and it shouldn't have been. But it was.

Two weeks later, Levi was startled when Dinah said, "I think I may have found a *Mann* I can trust."

They sat alone in the back room, eating the soup she'd made there. The back door stood open to let in the early summer breeze.

"What do you mean?" he asked, suddenly anxious for no reason, at all. "I didn't know you were driving out with someone new."

"Oh, you know him. Remember when I told you that Joel Woomert had taken me home?" She sent him a dimpled smile from her stool.

"Joel Woomert?" Levi echoed to buy time.

"*Yah.* We've been driving a half dozen times and he seems very nice. He asked me to drive out with only him."

Levi sent her an oblique glance. Although he'd always known Joel, he couldn't help remembering the *Mann's* arrogance when at the shop several weeks ago. That might have been a bad day for him. Everyone had them, after all.

"You remember Joel, don't you?"

Dinah looked so sweet and he hated to say anything to her about what he'd seen of Joel. He knew he'd decided not to say anything about it. Now, he didn't know what to do.

"I do." Levi feared his words sounded terse, but he didn't know what else to say.

She turned away from the makeshift kitchen to look at him where she'd been serving herself another bowl of soup. "You don't like Joel?"

Dodging the question, he cringed inside when he said, "I think it matters more if you like him."

He admitted to himself that he wasn't being totally honest with her.

"Joel seems pleasant enough…and he asked me to drive with him alone after only a short time."

"Well, that has to be nice after Bart's behavior."

"I hear it in your voice, though. You don't like Joel. What do you have against him?" Dinah persisted.

He really didn't want to say more, just adding, "You're the one driving out with him. You must like him."

She looked a little miffed, setting her bowl of soup on the kitchen counter with a thud before going to sit down in a huff. "If you have something against him, you should just say it."

Still, he hesitated.

"Levi! Out with it!"

Dinah didn't know why his opinion was so important, but it was. Somehow, they'd grown closer, working together.

His opinion was important. She found herself grieving that he wouldn't let himself be happy again.

"Alright," he said finally. "I've always thought a person's true self came out with store clerks and restaurant servers. You know, people who don't seem to matter much. And children. Have you seen him with children?"

"Of course, I have!" she said indignantly. "My youngest sister—Faith—is only fourteen. He's perfectly fine with her."

"Maybe so, but she's your sister," Levi also set his bowl down on the counter, "so I'm guessing Joel would be on his best behavior when he picks you up, and fourteen isn't really a *Kinder*."

"What are you saying? I think Joel's a good, trustworthy *Mann*. Don't you think I'm able to assess a *Mann* accurately?"

Dinah knew her voice had risen and that she sat straighter in her chair, but Levi's words—and what she could see by his expression—really annoyed her. It almost sounded like he didn't think she could assess character!

Never mind that she'd worried about this herself. A little voice in her head reminded her that she hadn't recognized Bart's true character, but she flew right past it.

Springing up from the chair, her cheeks hot, she faced him.

"You may not sometimes," Levi retorted, "see everything. You haven't been driving out with him all that long. Have you asked your *familye* what they think?"

"Of course!" Maybe she hadn't asked them in so many words, Dinah reflected, feeling ruffled, but she knew they'd have said something if they had doubts about Joel.

Surely.

"Abby would have told me if she saw a problem. Adam, too! Not to mention my *Mamm* and *Daed*."

Levi's attitude really made her blood boil! He seemed to think she wouldn't recognize an untrustworthy *Mann*!

"I haven't heard you say anything against Joel!" she spat out.

If she had to say at that moment why she was so mad at Levi, she couldn't, but Dinah didn't want to think of that right then.

He hesitated before saying, "No, you haven't. It's just that, when he stopped by here the other day, he was high-handed. Joel seemed arrogant and impatient."

"Seemed arrogant! Impatient!" Dinah said with disgust. "To who? To you? I believe you're making all this up."

"What?" he snapped. "Why would I do that? And I'd think you'd need more than a few buggy drives to decide who to trust and who not to trust?"

By this time, Levi had stepped forward, not two feet away from where she stood.

"So, you're saying that I don't know who is trustworthy and who isn't?"

They were practically yelling at one another by now.

He stabbed a finger at her. "You! You said as much! When you wanted me to help you decide! You haven't been able to pick a *Mann*! After all, you're the one who's been driving out with almost all the *Menner* in this town!"

Dinah quivered with rage. "How dare you? How dare you say that I can't decide who can and can't be trusted!"

"This is ridiculous!! I'm not the one recovering from having been rejected! You were planning to marry Bart and he dumped you!"

"No, you're the one hiding from ever being hurt again," she shot back. "You lost your wife and you don't want to risk again. I'm, at least, trying to find a new mate!"

The instant the words were out of her mouth, Dinah regretted them. The stricken look in Levi's eyes made her want to rush to take back what she'd said, but it was already out there.

And it was true.

For a moment, he just glowered at her. Then he said simply, "That may be, but it doesn't change your situation. You can't know that Joel can be trusted. You can't trust yourself to know that."

Dinah gasped, feeling tears prickling at the back of her eyes, and said "You are horrible! Everything that I thought about you! I quit! Do you hear? I quit!"

"I hear you," he said, his face still dark.

Turning to rush out of the shop, she found herself hoping desperately that she wasn't wrong about Joel and that Levi was.

CHAPTER TEN

"I don't know how the argument started!" Levi told Reuben at the shop the next day. "She said something about one of the *Menner* she's driving out with. I don't know."

"And you don't remember what she said?"

Levi did remember, but he just couldn't tell his friend exactly what Dinah said. Even though he was mad at her—and thought she was being foolish in her quick assessment of Joel—he didn't want to expose her. He trusted Reuben not to spread gossip, but Levi still didn't want…

He didn't know what he thought about this mess.

"I really appreciate you coming in to help this morning." His words were short, but he did welcome Reuben's being there. "I could have managed things myself, but it's always good to have your company."

Reuben shrugged. "Dinah quit. I wasn't about to leave you stranded. In fact, I'm surprised that Dinah Zook didn't give you a few days' notice. She seems like a reasonable girl."

The two men had met the afternoon before when Levi had closed the shop long enough to go into town and get a package of parts from the post office. Having run into his friend so soon after the blow up with Dinah, he'd naturally told Reuben that Dinah had quit.

"I'm glad your brothers can do your chores. I'd hate to put you out."

"*Yah*," Reuben said cheerfully. "That's one of the good things about working our farms together. That, and I like working with them. Able and Hiram are good fellows."

He sent Levi a searching look across the counter. "So, Dinah just got mad and left? That seems unlike her. She's usually such a reliable girl. Didn't you say she came to help on a Sunday when that bad storm sent a branch through the front window?"

After not responding for several seconds, Levi admitted. "Yes. She did do that and she's been reliable in every way."

He paused for a few more minutes, trying to find the right words. "We argued about our different views of a *Mann* she's driving out with several times."

Even as he admitted this, he knew Reuben would have questions.

"She talks to you about the *Menner* she's seeing?" his friend asked. "I'm surprised. This is usually something a *Maedel* would talk to her mother about."

Now that he'd started, Levi found the words tumbling out. "I know. A while back, I happened to be out with Dinah when we ran across Bart Altorfer and his new *Frau*."

"Oh." Reuben's one word was full of comprehension. "I see. You didn't live here when that all happened, did you?"

"No, but I did remember that Dinah and Bart had been seeing a lot of one another before I moved. As this kind of thing isn't discussed, I heard little. I was surprised that Dinah Zook hadn't married Bart, but he married, instead, a girl I'd never heard of."

Reuben nodded. "Tabitha Brandenberger's great uncle left her his farm."

"And farms are hard to come by," Levi agreed. "So, Bart chose to marry the girl with the farm. We saw them at a fair and Dinah was…"

Levi hesitated, remembering her distress. "She was very upset."

"I can imagine. I've always thought it is unfortunate that Bart settled here after he married, but the farm his wife inherited is here."

Releasing a deep breath, Levi said, "After I saw all that, Dinah and I just started talking about the *Menner* she's been considering. She's driven out with many. It didn't seem awkward. Her *familye* is naturally hesitant to say anything about her getting married. It's a sensitive subject anyway and was even worse after Bart married. She'd been ditched and she's wondered how to know who to trust."

"We knew, Rachel and I, that she's not married and we've prayed that Dinah will find the right *Mann* for her."

"I don't know that she's found him, though," Levi voiced abruptly. Seeing Reuben's inquiring gaze, he admitted, "She's driven out with Joel Woomert several times. He came to the shop the other day to buy several small things a week or so ago and, when he was here, he was…"

Trailing off, he tried to find the right word. "He was kind of a jerk. Arrogant and talking down to me. Anyway, when she came in here and said that she'd decided after only a few drives that he's trustworthy, I eventually told her about what I'd seen. She insisted, so I told her."

"Wow," Reuben responded. "Wow."

"I know, we aren't to judge others," Levi admitted, "and I thought that day that he might have just been in a bad mood. Then, she came in, saying she thought he was good and trustworthy."

"And you told her. Told her what exactly?"

"That maybe she'd hurried into deciding to trust him," Levi said, trying to explain. "I told her about Joel's behavior that day. I said maybe she didn't know him well enough yet to make that decision."

As he said it, Levi recognized how that must have sounded to Dinah. She already doubted herself and her ability to see character.

"Well," Reuben returned, "I can see how you must have argued."

"She has been talking to me about the *Menner* she sees!" Levi pointed out. "Telling her this isn't far from our discussions."

"Dinah didn't take your opinion on Joel well?"

Levi looked down. "No. She didn't. She even started talking about me, accusing me of being afraid to marry again!"

Reuben looked at him with compassion. "She said that, did she?"

"*Yah*! Like that has anything to do with her situation."

"It doesn't," Reuben agreed. "That being true, you did have it rough. Losing Anna that way."

"I think I'll always miss her," Levi volunteered after a silent moment. "That doesn't mean I won't carry on. I know that I must marry again—the bishop has been after me to do this—but this is a serious thing. One needs to consider carefully before joining for life with another person."

"Yes, absolutely." Reuben was quiet for several minutes. "You and Dinah are both doing this? Seriously considering who is best to marry?"

Levi stared at his friend. "I suppose so. I guess we are."

That same afternoon, Joel cheerfully remarked to Dinah, "I'm glad you're free to take a ride today."

"Yes," she said, "I haven't gotten home this early when I worked at Levi's shop," she responded in a subdued voice. Nothing about this seemed right and she'd found herself running over and over the fight she'd had with Levi.

Joel tapped the reins on the back of his buggy horse. "Well, he never was very friendly, from what I recall. From what I hear, Levi isn't easy to work with."

Out of the corner of her eye, Dinah observed that he seemed...unconcerned?

"I just don't know why he acted the way he did."

Taking a corner, Joel glanced at her, "*Neh*? Well, some people are just hard to get along with. Best not to worry about it."

It occurred to her that she and Levi had gotten along well, at least, once he'd apologized about what he said that hurt Abby.

She couldn't *not* worry about their argument, either.

"We always worked well together, even after that bad storm beat the place up." Dinah sighed.

Joel reached over—with a familiarity that was a little startling—to pat her knee. "There are plenty of jobs around and I bet your *Mamm* and *Grossmammi* are glad to have you home."

"I guess," Dinah said, realizing confiding in him didn't seem like the best idea, "although my sister, Abby, helps with the cooking and cleaning at home. My two younger sisters, too."

"That's right," Joel said, his voice holding a self-congratulatory tone. "When you marry and have your own home, your sisters will be there to help. Mary and Ruth, you said?"

"Naomi and Faith," she said, noting that he hadn't learned the younger girls' names.

"Hey," Joel said with a laugh, "I do remember that your brothers are Adam, Judah, Noah and…Eli?"

"Ezra," she said, conscious of a growing hollowness inside her midsection.

"Adam?" Dinah said later that evening.

"Yes?" Her brother looked up from the book he'd been reading on the kitchen table by the light of an oil lamp.

She came to sit down across from him. "This thing with Levi is troubling me."

"What? *Mamm* said that the two of you had a falling out and you'd quit working at his kick scooter shop."

"We did argue," she said, tracing the wood grain in the tabletop with one finger. "And I did quit."

Adam closed his book, having set a scrap of paper in as a place holder. "I thought the two of you were getting along well after he apologized for what he said about Gabe? It even seemed that you liked him."

"We were getting on well and I did like him," she admitted, "but he said some other things the other day and I got mad all over."

"About Gabe and Abby? What did he say?"

"No, not about them." Dinah sighed. "We were talking about the *Menner* I've been driving out with—"

"All of them?" her brother asked in a playful voice.

She made a face at him. "Not you, too?"

"Levi noticed?" Her brother asked.

Going back to tracing patterns in the tabletop, she admitted, "*Yah*. A while back, actually. He's been—well, helping me sort through things. Talking with me about my feelings and thoughts about the different *Menner*…until now."

"Until now?"

Looking up at Adam, Dinah said, "You know I've driven out with Joel Woomert several times?"

He nodded. "*Grossmammi* said something about that. If he's what you're looking for."

She looked at Adam, some note in his voice ringing in her ears.

"I'm not sure," Dinah said, glad to have been able to say the words out loud. "He seemed nice.at first, but…"

Adam met her gaze steadily. "You're not sure now?"

"I was," she insisted. "For a while. You know I've been trying to sort out this—knowing who to trust—since Bart chose to marry Tabitha? Levi's been a good sounding board. He really has and we could talk differently about all this because…all you here at home love me."

"We do," Adam confirmed.

She fell silent.

"Until Levi wasn't a good sounding board?" Adam prompted. "He said something about Joel?"

Dinah stirred in her seat, "*Yah*, but that wasn't the worst."

"Well, Joel's not perfect," her brother said finally, "but then none of us are. What did Levi say about him?"

Shaking her head, Dinah commented, "Levi said Joel was arrogant when he came into the shop, like Joel thought he didn't have to be nice to Levi—working there alone that day."

Adam nodded. "Sounds like Joel. He can be a *bisskatz*."

She fell silent again and when her brother said nothing, Dinah said, "Maybe. I don't know, but, like I said, that wasn't what really upset me."

She stopped for a moment. "I didn't know how to take it, but Levi then said something about me not knowing who to trust."

"Isn't that what you've been talking to him about?"

"Yes," she burst into speech, "I guess so, but he didn't have to say it like he thought I wasn't capable of recognizing who was trustworthy! Like he naturally knew better than I do! He doesn't! He shouldn't have said that. Particularly when I'd just told him that I thought I might be able to trust Joel…eventually."

Her brother nodded again. "I can see how that would upset you, but didn't you just tell me the other day that Levi was becoming a friend? And the two of you were getting along, working even better together? Weren't his words coming from a friend?"

"I did say that about him." It was her turn to look down, her chest hurting. "And we were. He seemed…different than I'd thought he was. At least, until now. His words about my not knowing who to trust didn't sound very friendly! I was starting to think Levi believed in me. That he thought I could sort this out."

"And now your friend is gone," Adam reflected slowly.

"It seems Levi was never truly my friend," she muttered in a bitter voice. "Not really."

Several days later, Levi stood alone at the counter in his shop, smoothing splinters off a board he planned to use for a toy.

The shop door stood open and, even though the summer had come, no *Kinder* were in the shop. He had no one working with him, as Reuben had to return to attend to his farm.

Levi told himself that he was fine.

His sister, Esther, had doubted that he could run the shop on his own, but this clearly wasn't the case.

Laying the sandpaper aside, he stared out the front window. If he ever needed help, he knew there would eventually be someone in the community to help. It just wouldn't be Dinah.

Entangled in his thoughts, he propped sandy hands in front of him on the counter.

How did he fix this mess? Returning to the events that kept circling in his head, he thought of that last conversation with her. How had things gotten so twisted? He'd been focused on helping her. Dinah's buggy rides with the different *Menner* in town hadn't gotten her anywhere and-and he'd just wanted to help.

She'd gone through such a hard time after that *Schlang*, Bart, had treated her so badly. How could she have ever spent so much time with the snake? Dinah deserved so much better.

Levi looked ahead without seeing, his thoughts tumbling around.

Dear Gott, he prayed, *help me. I don't know what to do, but this situation has gone so terribly wrong. How do I make peace with Dinah? I want so much to make peace with her! You've told us to love our brethren. To be kind to one another. I know I shouldn't have said that she hadn't judged Joel right, but what was I to do? Let her marry this very wrong Mann?*

Should I have stayed out of the whole mess? Maybe never gotten so...close with her?

Levi stopped then, so struck by a sudden thought that had descended into his head.

He didn't want her to find another *Mann*! That's why it was so clear to him that Joel wasn't right for her!

Still staring ahead, he paused, the realization that had just popped into his thoughts, like it had been inserted into his head in golden letters! *Gott*? Maybe this was the answer to his prayers?

Maybe he wanted to be Dinah's *Mann*! Risking love with her would be worth it.

CHAPTER ELEVEN

"I'm so glad you're feeling better and that you came by to visit," Dinah told Becca the next day. While their *Mamm* and *Grossmammi* were inside the *Haus*, preparing lunch, the girls worked at different tasks around the yard.

Abby pulled weeds around the flourishing plants in the kitchen garden while Naomi and Faith pumped water to sprinkle along the rows there.

"*Denki*!" Her younger sister smiled happily back. Even though she was the fourth in the *familye*—and a year younger than Dinah—Becca had always been the most out-going of the older girls.

"Saul was lucky when he won you," Abby observed from where she cleared weeds along the rows, so the vegetables growing in the garden got all the nutrition from the earth.

"That's so sweet of you!" Becca braced two hands at the sides of the bins.

Raking up the leaves blown into corners and under shrubs, left over from the winter winds, Dinah moved toward where Becca held the bin to hold them. She needed to keep busy and was glad of the task. Otherwise, her thoughts just strayed back to the fight with Levi and nothing was to be gained from replaying this again.

Instead, she reflected that the leaves would go nicely in the compost mound behind the barn to make nourishment for the garden when they were broken down.

Above, the sun shone a cheerful yellow in a blue sky and summer-warm breezes blew gently through the yard. Their brothers had all gone to work in the fields with *Daed*, joined even by young Ezra now that he'd finished school.

"So, Abby," Becca called out in a teasing voice, "Saul said the new *Mann* in town—Eli Probst—told him you are spicy!"

"What?" Their oldest sister responded, her normally calm voice sharp.

"Eli Probst," Becca said again.

"Who is he?" Dinah knew she shouldn't pursue this, particularly since she got the impression that Abby had heard very well what Becca said the first time.

Abby ducked behind a particularly thick tomato plant. "I can't hear you."

"Of course, she can't," Becca said, laughter in her voice.

"Who is he?" Dinah hissed this time.

"Eli Probst came to drill our new well. Saul noticed the other one isn't producing as much water and Eli is apparently the *Mann* everyone has dig their wells.

"He's a young *Mann*?" asked Dinah, because there was no missing the meaning behind Becca's teasing.

Abby emerged from the tomato plant to say tartly, "*Neh*. Not really, and he acts like God gave him as a gift to us all!"

Dinah stopped raking to look at her sister. "If he's digging a well at Saul and Becca's, how did you meet him?"

Having brought the water buckets to the garden with Faith, Naomi said, "We had a well drilled a couple of years back and the *Mann* who did that for *Daed* was old. Older than *Daed*."

"Eli took over his father's business several years ago," Becca said. "Apparently, he was one of the workers before that."

"Where did you meet this Eli, Abby?" Dinah guessed she should have been used to having to repeat questions, having grown up in a large *familye*.

"I saw him at the hardware store first a few weeks ago." Abby's words were cool and brief. "Then, *Mamm* sent me to Becca's with the stew she'd made last Wednesday."

"That was before your fight with Levi," Faith said. "You were still working at his shop."

"Thank you." Dinah couldn't help the sarcastic note in her voice. Like she needed reminding!

"What happened that Eli whatever-his-name saw that you can be spicy?" Naomi looked up from drizzling water along the garden row.

"Nothing!" The tart note was in Abby's voice again.

"Sister," Dinah chided.

"He happened to come around their *Haus* when I drove up in the buggy," Abby returned after a few minutes.

"And?" Becca was obviously enjoying this.

"I had everything under control."

"Of course, you did," Naomi said. "You always do. What did you have under control?"

"Well, I did this time." Their older sister said defensively. "I didn't need his help."

"Because you never need help," Becca said in a barely-audible voice.

"What did he do?" Dinah felt there was more to the story. Ever since Gabe died, she'd felt a little protective of Abby.

"He kept trying to carry the stew inside!"

This didn't sound so alarming to Dinah, but she knew Abby always liked to be strong and not need help. It made her sister very difficult to help, sometimes.

"And you thought you could manage on your own." Becca had set down the bin and come to lean against post helping to hold the fence around the garden.

The scenario was coming clear now to Dinah, who stood leaning on the rake next to the garden fence.

"Was the stew in *Mamm's* heavy iron pot?" Faith piped up to ask.

"It was, but I can carry the pot. It was very secure on the buggy floor."

"Eli saw you struggling to pick it up, didn't he?" Becca asked. "He told Saul something like that."

"I wasn't struggling!" Abby hotly rejected the inference that she'd been having a hard time.

Naomi asked, seeming to know the answer. "You said something to him about not needing his help, right?"

"What makes you assume that?" Abby sidestepped the question.

"Because you do the same when one of us offers you any help," their youngest sister said.

"He was a stranger!" Abby defended. "And if I'd needed help, I would have taken some of my other bundles in first."

"But, you probably didn't." Dinah grimaced at her sister.

"That's when Eli got a taste of your spiciness." Becca chuckled.

"I was fine," Abby said firmly. "Anyway, Dinah's the one with a new beau. We don't need to talk about me."

"*Grossmammie* has said," Naomi responded in a firm voice belied by her twinkling smile, "that we are, none of us, to talk about others' lives. We aren't to comment on who Dinah drives out with."

Dinah sat down on an overturned bucket, giving a sigh. "I appreciate that and the *Ordnung* has directed us to be private about matters of the heart, but I am all mixed up. I'd appreciate being able to talk about it."

Of course, if she were still working with Levi, she'd talk to him about her experience. Since, he thought her incapable, however, she still felt hurt. And she missed him.

For a second, an image of his smile as he stood at his work bench flickered in Dinah's mind.

She shook her head then, determined to push the *Mann* out of her memory!

"Haven't you been driving out with lots of *Buwes*?" Becca took the bucket Faith had cast aside and turned it over for a seat next to Dinah.

She looked down, "*Yah*. Before I started driving out with Joel Woomert."

"And now you only drive out with Joel?" Her sister sent her a twinkling smile.

"I saw her leaving with him the other day," Faith stuck in.

"Just him these last few weeks, but I'm pretty sure it doesn't mean anything," Dinah said.

She looked down at the rich, brown dirt in the garden, freshly turned by Abby's spade. She felt a growing uneasiness with Joel. His cheerful lack of response to her distress about her argument with Levi seemed less like encouragement than a general disregard of her. How could he not care about something so important to her?

She'd hate if she was wrong about Joel and Levi was right, but more than that, she hated that she couldn't talk to Levi about this. She hated, too, that she wanted to talk to the *Schlang*, at all!

Levi drew in a breath sharply. He'd known he'd see Dinah at their next church meeting, but he hadn't clearly thought out that she might be sitting with Joel Woomert.

Joel didn't deserve her. The thought streaked through his head.

Tables had been set outside the *Haus* for the meal after their services. There she sat, next to Joel, her black *Kapp* leaning close to him to hear something he said.

Their closeness sent a shaft of pain through Levi. He sent up a quick prayer to *Gott* to help him deal with this distress.

He hadn't expected to feel this when he saw her, but now the sweet turn of her cheek and the glimmer of a smile on her rosy lips made Levi turn to stone, just looking at Dinah.

Dear Gott, he prayed silently, *help me. I...I hate this, Lord. Hate that she and I are at odds. Hate that I made this broken mess. I said all the wrong things and I don't know how to fix this.*

It came to him all of the sudden that he needed to find Dinah's sister. He'd made that comment about Gabe having died without *Kinder* out of his own grief and he'd been wrong. He needed to tell this to Abigail Eichelberger. He owed her an apology and he didn't think he'd offered one sincere enough.

Winding his way through people chattering as they stood between the tables in the crowded yard, he searched for Dinah's sister. Finally, he saw her talking to several *Frau* close to her age, one with a *Boppli* clinging to her skirt.

"May I speak to you, please," Levi asked Abby Eichelberger when there was a pause in the conversation.

An unreadable expression on her face, Abigail turned to him.

"I owe you an apology," he said in a low voice.

A small frown wrinkled her forehead. "For what?"

"I apologized before," he said, still talking quietly as her friends chattered several feet away, "but I want to say again how foolish it was of me to have said what I said of Gabe. I know my friend was very happy with you and my words came out of my own trouble."

She looked at him, her expression not changing. "That is as may be. We are beyond what you said that day."

"Then, I am forgiven for my hasty speech?"

"That's between you and *Gott*," Abigail said in an angry tone, "but I've yet to forgive you for what you said to Dinah the other day!"

Levi felt his jaw drop. He snapped it shut, asking, "What? What did I say to Dinah?"

He knew, though, their interaction that day was burned into his memory. He felt shamed by it, but her words of interest in Joel had spurred Levi into ugly speech. This was no excuse, but it was true.

"I think you do know!" Abby Eichelberger snapped, "and you should apologize to her for saying she couldn't be trusted to pick a *Mann*. My sister is the best thing that happened to your shop or to you. There is far more need for you to apologize to her than to do so again to me!"

"There you are," Joel said at the meal after the next church meeting, shifting to face the table. Several of his friends had been standing there talking to him, and Dinah recognized among them were *Menner* she'd driven home with.

Of course, their community was smaller and it was to be expected that she'd have contact with *Menner* that she'd passed on, but she felt a flush of heat in her cheeks, all the same.

Dinah sent the three men a forced smile. She'd gone to school with them all and this made the moment even more awkward.

"*Denki* for the food," Joel said casually, opening a napkin and shoving in the neck of his shirt.

He looked up at her, "Is there a drink to go with all this food?"

Having brought him a plate of food—after he requested she do this—Dinah registered that Joel had almost an air of ownership when he spoke to her.

"*Yah.* Would you like me to bring you a cup of drink?"

It would have been natural to do the same for any member of their church. She was used to serving food for the after church meal, but Joel's manner seemed too sure of himself and it just lined up with everything she'd been noticing about him recently.

She was sadly more and more convinced that Joel Woomert wasn't the right *Mann* for her. Just as Levi had said.

Maybe Levi was right about her, too, she thought.

Later that afternoon, standing beside Joel's buggy, she said, "*Neh.* You don't need to drive me home. I'm leaving with my *familye.*"

Having paused in the act of climbing into the driver's seat, Joel turned to stare at her. "You are?"

This was more difficult than she'd thought, Dinah reflected internally. She'd never before broken things off with a *Mann.* She'd been broken up with, but she'd never done it herself. She'd spent years courting with Bart before he dumped her to marry Tabitha. That she'd only been driving out with Joel a few weeks should have made this less awkward.

"Joel,' she said in a firm voice, "I don't think we should drive out together anymore. I don't think I'm the girl for you and you're definitely not the *Mann* for me."

She knew who was the *Mann* for her, but Levi had already told her he wasn't looking to love again.

"I thought you said Joel was the one." Abby commented as the girls lounged in their bedroom that afternoon before it was time to get supper started.

"I said I thought he could be the one," Dinah responded defensively, not looking at anyone directly. She felt foolish to have been so deceived.

Becca grinned. "This is better than most visits home."

"Why are you here?" Naomi questioned with a little of Abby's directness.

Dinah frowned at her. "Not that you aren't always welcome."

"Of course, we're glad to see you," Naomi chimed in hastily.

"I want to hear about Dinah having ended her courtship with Joel," her sister dodged.

Abby ignored this interchange to return to the subject. "You said that you were enjoying driving out with Joel. I remember this distinctly and you were upset with what Levi said about you not being able to recognize a *gut Mann*."

Drawing a deep breath, Dinah said, "Yes, I did tell you all that, but I also said that my driving out with him didn't mean anything."

"Of course, it means something," Becca insisted. "It always means something when a *Maedel* drives out with the same boy."

"And only that boy," Naomi added. "You said that you were driving out with only him."

"You also said you were hurt by what Levi said." Abby stressed this, faint redness blooming in her cheeks. "You were upset! I told Levi that he owed you an apology!"

"You did?" Dinah was astonished. "When? And why?"

"Because he hurt you! You're not the only one to worry about her sister." Abby stared at her a shade indignantly.

"Way better than most visits home." Becca squirmed enthusiastically on Dinah's bed.

Needing a moment to process Abby having said this to Levi, Dinah said, "Why are you here when we saw you at the service just this morning?"

"Isn't there a Sing later tonight? I thought you'd be getting ready to go."

"Becca," Naomi stared at the sister only a little older than her. "You must have a reason for coming."

This time it was Becca who sounded defensive, although her cheeks bloomed even pinker than Abby's had. "I want to talk to *Mamm*, that's all. The services are always so crowded and busy there's no time to talk."

"You've already told us you're with child," Naomi said in a matter-of-fact voice.

Dinah squinted at Becca, trying to decide what she saw in her sister's face.

"Have you seen the midwife? It's definitely confirmed?" Abby reached over to lay her hand warmly over Becca's. "Why didn't you say so?"

"Oh, Becca, how wonderful!" Dinah chimed in with enthusiasm.

Becca put her other hand over Abby's. "I always think we shouldn't talk about this with you. Are you sure you're okay with this? Saul and I haven't been married very long."

"Long enough," Naomi chuckled.

"Of course, I'm okay!" Abby admonished her. "More than okay. Very, very happy. Do you think I want you cheated of this gift from *Gott*?"

"Well," Dinah observed, after hugging her younger sister, "I understand why she's worried about your feelings."

"Don't be silly," Abby insisted. "This is a joy and, besides, families all around me are getting bigger."

"I know," Dinah said, "but this has been a big heartache for you, not having Gabe's *Kinder*."

"You know you've mourned it," Naomi said, sending her sister a compassionate look.

"I have, but that doesn't mean I want any of you to share in my same grief. Of course, you'll have children. It's as *Gott* intended." Abby looked over to Dinah. "Now that this is settled, are you sure about Joel? What happened to change your mind?"

"I have one more bit of news," Becca interrupted.

"You do?" Dinah asked, startled.

"*Yah*." Her pregnant sister seemed shy. "The midwife thinks we're having twins. She heard two heartbeats."

The room broke out in bedlam, her four sisters shrieking and gathering around to hug Becca.

"Twins," Abby said in a dazed voice. "Wow."

After the many comments and questions that followed Becca's news, the sisters subsided enough for Abby to once again ask Dinah, "So, you're sure that you don't think Joel Woomert is the *Mann* for you?"

"I'm sure," she confirmed. "He didn't seem so in the beginning, but he started to get...comfortable with me. Almost as if he took it for granted that I'd become his *Frau*. As though, I belonged to him. Cocky and sure of himself, like he'd won a prize or something."

"After only driving out a few weeks?" Naomi asked. "*Daed* and *Mamm* have been married nearly thirty years and he still doesn't seem to take her for granted."

Dinah nodded. "Exactly. I want a *Mann* to love me like that."

"You deserve that," Abby said, "and more. I probably shouldn't have been so mean to Levi. Although, he still had no right to speak to you that way."

CHAPTER TWELVE

Dinah wondered, at the Sing the next weekend, how she could ever have thought Joel might be the *Mann* for her. No doubt, some girls would be glad of his attentions, but she must have been out of her mind.

Across the room, Joel guffawed at some stupid remark he'd made, several other *Menner* laughing with him.

Now that Naomi had gone off with her friend, Mary Souder, and Abby to help in the kitchen, since the singing was over, Dinah sat alone.

Her older sister went back and forth, putting out plates of cookies and treats on the table while friends chatted in clumps around the room.

Painfully aware of Levi's voice as he spoke to Jakob Bachman in the dining room, Dinah felt her heart squeeze in her chest. She missed Levi, even though she had reason to be upset with him. He never should have spoken to her as he did.

"Dinah!"

She whipped around to see Esther, Levi's sister and her good friend, standing in front of her.

"Esther!" Dinah hugged her friend. "I didn't know you were visiting!"

"*Yah*," her friend said cheerfully, "Jakob and I came in this afternoon. Our buggy broke down yesterday and we got here as quickly as we could after Jakob fixed it, but we were too late for the service."

Hugging her again, Dinah exclaimed, "It is so nice to see you."

Esther made a face. "I hear you're no longer working with Levi."

Her happiness at seeing her friend withered in the face of this distressing reality. Dinah stiffly said, "*Neh.*"

She swallowed and stretched her lips into what she feared was a travesty of a smile, tears prickling at the back of her eyes.

"It is no matter, friend," Esther said, pressing Dinah's hand with hers. "We don't need to talk about whatever happened. Levi didn't have anything to say about this, either, other than to the fact that you no longer worked with him."

"Esther," Dinah asked her friend suddenly, as if they'd moved on to another subject, "what do you think of marrying a *Mann* who tells you that he doesn't want to love again. A *Mann* who said he only wanted a wife to make a *familye*, as *Gott* wants. That would be his only reason to take a *Frau*."

Dinah felt herself flush as she asked the question.

After a moment, Esther responded in a careful tone, "And this *Mann* outright says he doesn't love the *Maedel* in question?"

"Yes," Dinah responded, hoping her cheeks weren't bright red.

"Well, then, I could understand a *Maedel* refusing him…unless this is the kind of marriage she wants. Some women want even this kind of *familye*, if having a home and *Kinder* isn't available any other way."

"They do," Dinah said gloomily. Levi could certainly find a *Frau* who'd accept his offer. Not easily, perhaps, but he'd find one. She tried to cling to her indignation that he'd thought this of her, although all she felt was heartbroken that she might live to see him married to another woman.

"I know you won't have to accept this kind of offer," her friend said after several more moments, giving her a hug. "I know you'll find a *Mann* who loves you and who you love, as much."

"*Denki*," Dinah managed, not as convinced as Esther. She already loved a *Mann*, who was determined to protect his heart and who thought her unable to make a heart-decision anyway. "*Denki*."

"What happened between you two? Talk." Esther ordered her brother two days after the Sing. "This has gone on too long. I saw Dinah yesterday and she wasn't herself. I know she doesn't work for you anymore, but she wouldn't tell me why."

On the front porch with his sister before heading to the shop, Levi could only say with difficulty, "We got into a disagreement over the *Mann* she's been driving out with."

The rest of his feelings and the situation with Dinah were just too big. Not since Anna died had he been so drawn to a *Maedel*. Nothing about this, though, seemed clear. He acknowledged now to himself that he loved her, but, with his hasty words about her, he'd hurt Dinah. He didn't know how to fix this.

Esther frowned. "We aren't to talk about such things, who drives out with who. You know that. How did this even come up?"

Levi felt himself flush. "Dinah has gotten into the habit of talking to me of the different *Menner* she drives out with."

His sister's mouth dropped open.

"She has? She did?"

"You know that Bart dumped her and married—"

"—Tabitha Brandenberg. *Yah*. That happened before I married Jakob and we moved away."

"Well, since then, she's not settled on another *Mann*, although many have driven her home from services and Sings."

Esther nodded. "*Yah*? I knew that. So, why did she talk with you about it?"

Levi took a breath, trying to drag his thoughts together.

"I recall that she wasn't keen on the idea of working with you. She refused at first." Esther hesitated. "She said you were rude and cold. Unfriendly and something about you having hurt her sister? I didn't understand it all, but she felt strongly about it. What did you say about her beau?"

Her words hurt and Levi rushed to defend himself. "Nothing that wasn't true! I said he wasn't kind when he came here, acting arrogant and all. He did!"

"Hmmm, she usually has such good judgment, but I know the situation with Bart surprised her. Well, it surprised us all!"

Lifting his chin to look her in the eye, Levi confessed, "I was…upset when she didn't listen to me about Joel—the *Mann* she's been driving out with—and…."

"And?"

Levi responded to her prompting question, "And I said that she doesn't know who is trustworthy and who isn't."

"You said that?" Esther looked appalled. "After her being mistaken about Bart?"

"She hasn't had a lot of interaction with this Joel. They've only been driving out a while and although we all went to school together, she is younger than him and didn't spend any real time with him."

Levi's chest felt as if he'd been running a long while, even though he and Esther sat still on the porch.

"But you and Joel Woomert were in the same grade. *Yah*? You spent time around him," his sister pointed out shrewdly. "He was still arrogant when he came to the shop?"

"Yes, he was." Levi knew absolutely what happened that day with Joel, but Joel didn't seem the biggest issue, right now. Dinah thought Levi was cold and unfriendly?

Esther lifted her brows as she shrugged. "That's a sin in *Gott's* eyes, but He knows the heart, not us."

"Still, we are to choose mates that make us better and bring us to *Gott*." Levi knew Dinah made him better. Made him stronger and…had healed his damaged heart. He loved her, but perhaps she didn't feel the same.

"Yes, but we don't know the heart and you shouldn't have said Dinah couldn't decide herself who to trust."

"I know." Levi tightened his jaw. "I know. It's not true and now she won't even speak to me.".

"I need to speak to you, Levi Becker."

A week later, he looked up from his workbench to see Abigail Eichelberger standing in the shop.

Levi put down his tools and wiped the grease from his hands as he went over to where Abigail stood at the counter. "*Goedemorgen*, *Frau* Eichelberger. I am happy to speak about anything with you."

He looked into Dinah's sister's face, her blue gaze stern.

It was earlyish in the morning and the shop was empty of customers. Sunlight streamed through the front window, lighting up the whole room.

"I need to tell you something that I wouldn't normally mention," she said.

"Okay."

Abigail looked down at the high counter between them, as if trying to decide what to say.

"Are you alright, *Frau*?"

Glancing up, Abigail said bluntly, "*Yah*, but Dinah is not."

"What do you mean? Is she sick?" Levi took a step closer to the counter, grabbing at the edge. "I saw her briefly at the last Sing. She seemed fine."

"She isn't," Abigail enunciated crisply.

Still gripping the edge of the counter, he made himself say, "Perhaps you should tell Joel Woomert, if she's unwell. She might prefer that you speak with him."

The thought of Dinah sick or in need had every fiber in him tensed, but he, as much as he hated it, he knew he needed to let her choice of *Mann* address this.

Abigail waved her hand dismissively. "She ended the thing with Joel at that Sing weeks ago. She doesn't want him."

"Truly?" Levi glanced up to look at her keenly. He was afraid to believe her words. "She said this to you?"

"Yes, truly. He's a *Bisskatz* and she got tired of him acting already like she belonged to him."

Levi felt relief flooding through his body. "I'm glad. Very glad."

"Well, you need to be more than that." Her words were crisp again. "Fix this thing between you and Dinah. She's unhappy and it shows. Moping around all the time. It's been hard to watch."

"What do you mean? I can't do anything. She won't even talk to me."

"Then, you do the talking," Abigail recommended tartly. "From the little she's said about your fight, you need to grovel a little. Apologize. You're good at that."

He reluctantly laughed at that. "*Denki.* Yes, I need to do that. In our last conversation, I said at least one thing I shouldn't have."

"You did. Tell her now and don't wait any longer."

Frowning, Levi asked, "Why? I mean what is the hurry?"

"Because Dinah is miserable?" Abigail snapped, "and I hate her being so upset?"

"Oh."

"She loves you." There was absolute certainty in her words. "For whatever reason, you've lucked out. Dinah loves you."

Moving quickly around the counter to face her, Levi said with intensity, "Really? You think so? If that's so, I really have lucked out. I'm not sure how to get her to listen, though."

He thought a moment before asking. "Has she taken another job? Is she still home most days?"

"She's not taken another job and, *yah*, she's home most days." Abigail nodded.

"Good," Levi said, "I need to see her."

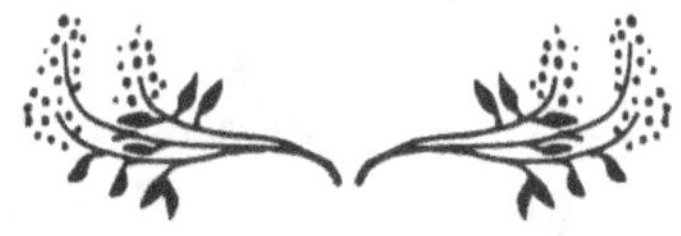

Two days later, Dinah stood before the clothesline, her back to the *Haus*, tears streaming down her face. She surreptitiously wiped at them with her sleeve. It was no good to go on mourning Levi.

No good, either, to keep driving out with random *Menner*, hoping that she'd find the right *Mann* for her. There was no doubt in her mind that she'd already found the *Mann* she loved.

Levi just didn't love her. Why that was why he'd asked her to marry him all those weeks ago. He had sworn off risking his heart and he didn't worry about that with her.

Dinah sniffed and went on draping wet clothes over the line, securing these with wooden pins that she shoved viciously over the wet fabric.

Birds sang out overhead and she could hear her youngest brother, Ezra, in the barn, talking to a chicken that had apparently strayed in there. Between these sounds, silence surrounded her and her throat hurt from the lump there.

It all didn't matter. As far as she could see, she thought, nothing really mattered.

Used to the chickens rustling through the grass in the yard, she didn't attend to shuffling behind her. Ezra must have shooed the chicken out of the barn.

"Ahem."

Lifting her head at the sound behind her of clearing a throat, Dinah scrubbed quickly at her face before turning around.

There, not three feet away, stood Levi, his head bare, his hat in his hand.

"*Hallo*," he said. "Are you doing well?"

"Levi!"

His answering smile was tentative, as if he weren't sure of his welcome. He cleared his throat again. "I've missed you."

"You have?" She probably sounded dim, but she was shocked to see him here in her backyard. Church, yes, but here?

She took a breath and then the question seemed worth asking. "Why are you here?"

Levi glanced quickly at the ground and then lifted his head to look directly at her. "I came to see you, of course."

He said this as though the reason for his presence here was obvious.

"Why?" she said, breaking the short silence between them.

The damp sheet she'd just hung on the line brushed against her as a gentle breeze came through the yard.

"I need to apologize," he said.

Honesty compelled her to say, "I think we were both in the wrong."

Levi blinked at this, but he hurried to add, "I never should have said anything about Joel—"

"You were right about him," she said calmly. "He is a jerk sometimes and he does ignore people he doesn't think are important."

"Oh."

"I broke up with him for that and other reasons. He started taking me for granted—ordering me around like we were already married. My *Daed* doesn't order my *Mamm* around, even now. Joel is nothing like *Daed*."

"I'm glad to hear it."

She stared at Levi. "You are?"

"I am." He shifted his hat to his other hand and came closer.

Dinah wasn't sure what to say.

Stepping forward, he stopped right in front of her. "I didn't mean what I said about you not knowing who to trust. I was just jealous of Joel."

"Of Joel?" she echoed, not understanding how this could be.

"*Yah*." Levi looked down again before glancing up at her. "I don't like Joel Woomert, Dinah, but that wasn't why I said what I said about you."

"It wasn't?" Holding her breath at the warmth in his gaze, she felt herself starting to tremble.

"No. I don't know exactly when this happened, but I've realized that I don't want to be afraid anymore." Levi reached to take her hand in his. "I am afraid, but I don't want to feel fear with anyone, but you."

This so startled her—along with the warmth of his fingers clasping hers—that Dinah just gulped. Then, compelled to ask the question, she started, "You asked me to marry you before—"

"I did," Levi broke in to say, "but what I offered wasn't fair to you. To either of us."

Dinah drew in a deep breath and let it out, profoundly conscious that he still held her hand. They stood like this, still beside the clothesline, sheets flapping in the breeze.

"And now?"

"Now, I know that I don't want to be afraid with anyone, but you. Just you, Dinah. That's why I got so upset when you told me you thought you could trust Joel. Yes, he is a jerk—"

"He is," she assured Levi.

"I know, but I would be happy seeing him with any other *Maedel*. Just not you."

"Oh!"

"Marry me, Dinah," he said in an unsteady voice. "Marry me, for real. All in. Everything."

"Are you sure? You've said many times that you don't want to risk loss again."

He pulled her into his arms. "You're worth the risk!"

He kissed her, then, despite the chickens now milling at their feet. Dinah gave up trying to reason with Levi and sank into his arms to kiss him back.

Thanks so much for purchasing Dinah's Darling! If you enjoyed this book, please consider leaving a review for Dinah's Darling, Book 2, Amish Sisters Marry Romance Series! Authors live and die by reviews and I would be very grateful if you would do me the honor of leaving one. Thanks in advance. I so appreciate it!

Glossary of Amish Terms:

Amische—how the Amish refer to themselves
Bickle—pickle
Bisskatz—skunk
Bopplin—babies
Bruder—brother
Buwe—boy
Daed—dad
Deerich—silly, idiotic, foolish
Eldre—parents
Englischer—anyone who isn't Amish
Familye—family
Frau—wife
Geschwischder—Brothers and sister
Gmay—church group that worship together
Goedenavond—good evening
Goedemorgen—good morning
Gott—God
Grank—sick
Grossdaddi—Grandfather
Grossmammi—Grandmother
Gut—good
Haus—house
Heiser—houses
Kinder/Kinner—children
Liebling—sweetheart, darling, honey
Maedel—young woman
Mamm—mother
Mann—man
Menner—men
Narrish—crazy
Neh—no
Schweschder—sister
Schmaert—smart
Schlang—snake
Yah—yes

About the Author

Rose Doss is an award-winning romance author. She has written thirty-one romance novels. Her books have won numerous awards, including a final in the prestigious Romance Writers of America Golden Heart Award.

A frequent speaker at writers' groups and conferences, she has taught workshops on characterization and, creating and resolving conflict. She works full time as a therapist.

Her husband and she married when she was only nineteen and he was barely twenty-one, proving that early marriage can make it, but only if you're really lucky and very persistent. They went through college and grad school together. She not only loves him still, all these years later, and she still likes him—which she says is sometimes harder. They have two funny, intelligent and highly accomplished daughters and three granddaughters, whose names all start with E like their great-grandmother, Eloise.

Rose loves writing and hopes you enjoy reading her work.

Amish Romances:

Amish By Choice (Amish Vows Romance, Prequel)
Amish Renegade (Amish Vows Romance, Bk 1)
Amish Princess (Amish Vows Romance, Bk 2)
Amish Heartbreaker (Amish Vows Romance, Bk 3)
Amish Spinster (Amish Vows Romance, Bk 4)
Amish Prodigal (Amish Vows Romance, Bk 5)
Amish Rogue (Amish Vows Romance, Bk 6)

Becca's Boy (Amish Sisters Marry Romance, Bk 1)
Dinah's Darling (Amish Sisters Marry Romance, Bk 2)
Abigail's Admirer (Amish Sisters Marry Romance, Bk 3)

www.rosedoss.com
www.twitter.com - carolrose@carolrosebooks
https://www.facebook.com/carol.rose.author

www.ingramcontent.com/pod-product-compliance
Lightning Source LLC
Chambersburg PA
CBHW072240190626
46809CB00018B/2860

* 9 7 8 1 9 5 5 9 4 5 5 2 3 *